The Contactees Die Young

Antoinette Azolakov

BANNED BOOKS
Austin, Texas

A Banned Book

FIRST EDITION

Copyright © 1989
By Antoinette Azolakov

Published in the United States of America
By Edward-William Publishing Company
Number 231, P.O. Box 33280, Austin, Texas 78764

ISBN 0-934411-18-2

To Beth O'Neal

Other books by Antoinette Azolakov

- **Cass and the Stone Butch**
- **Skiptrace**

Chapter 1

Whitney had the dream again and woke up screaming. It had all been there, just as it always was, peaceful
at first—the brown pine needles under her bare feet, the
summer heat, the stillness, the heaviness in the atmosphere, the huge trees towering over her little-girl head.
Then came the growing dread, the certainty that something unspeakably horrible was about to happen. Her heart
started to knock in her chest, the pulse to pound in her
ears.

Frightened and alone, she hid behind the trunk of a
gigantic pine, pressing herself tightly against the rough
bark, as slowly she became aware of the sound. It was
faint at first, only a murmur, but it rose to an all-pervasive
roar that overwhelmed the other senses until even thought
was impossible. She shut her eyes and clung to the tree,
terror leaping in her mind, animal hysteria welling up in
her until the roar of the sound was all but drowned in the
roar of her racing blood. And now with the sound came
the light—brilliant, blinding, brighter than the sun, sear-
ing through her tight-shut eyelids. Panicking, terrified, she
used the last of her conscious control to will herself to
move, to run, to get away, but her limbs felt like lead, her
legs did not respond, and she stood transfixed and helpless, a small, trapped animal, totally exposed—and
doomed.

☆ ☆ ☆

"T.D., I think I'm crazy." Whitney Way, long-legged
and tanned to the picture of youthful summertime fitness,

1

sat sprawled on the couch opposite my chair, one foot on the floor and the other leg up on the cushions. It was a position which, taken alone, might indicate relaxation and comfort with what she was telling me, but her arms were tight against her body and her hands were clasped together in her lap, a furrow of tension creasing the center of her forehead: trying to look cool and not succeeding.

"What makes you think that?" I watched the frown lines tighten as her eyes wandered the wall of my office behind my left shoulder. Their focus and movement told me she was reading my diploma, as if the information that Tahoka Daisy Renfro had received her doctorate in psychology from The University of Texas was news to her. I waited. The intelligent brown eyes cut suddenly back and met my own defiantly.

"I think —" she began resolutely, but then resolve wavered and her glance veered away to the wall again. She was silent. I let her struggle with it.

"I think, when I was a little girl . . ." Her eyes came back to mine with a visible effort. Her breathing was quick and shallow, tension radiating from her, and even her skin color seemed to pale. Whatever this was, Whitney wasn't having an easy time getting it out. "When I was a little girl, maybe just about five or six, I think I was picked up by a UFO."

I raised my eyebrows and looked interested.

The story came out in a rush. "I've had a recurring dream all my life. I never thought about telling you about it, because it was just a nightmare. Well, not just a nightmare. An awful nightmare. I guess I put it out of my mind right after it happened every time, because it's just too frightening or something. Anyway, in this dream I'm a little girl out in the woods, I guess it's near our house in East Texas where we lived until I was about ten."

I nodded to confirm that I remembered that basic fact of her history. Whitney had been my client for several months now, working through some conflicts arising from internalized homophobia, not an unusual problem among lesbian and gay clients. It's hard to let go of the attitudes you're brought up with, even when you know they're wrong.

Encouraged by my nod, Whitney went on. "Anyway, in the dream I get to feeling scared, really terrified, and I know something awful is going to happen. But what happens is just a roaring noise and a very bright light, and I try to run and I can't move. It's like I'm paralyzed, just rooted to the spot."

"And then what happens?"

"Nothing. I wake up. My heart's beating like a trip hammer and I feel like I've had an electric shock or something. Tingly all over, in a very unpleasant way. Scared to death. Only last night when I had it, I woke up screaming."

"It sounds very frightening."

"It is."

"So what do you make of this?"

"I know it sounds crazy. But I really think I'm remembering a UFO encounter." Her eyes took on a pleading look. "God, it sounds so stupid to say that! I've always laughed at people that said things like that. But I think it *happened* to me. Or maybe not; maybe it's just a dream. Maybe it's just some fear I've had that's coming out like this." She lapsed into silence again, still so tense I could almost see her shaking.

"What do you think happened?" I kept my voice calm and neutral, just asking for information, carefully not reacting to the UFO claim.

"I don't know. God, T.D., I don't know!" She looked down at her hands, pulled them apart with an effort, then sat up straight and slapped her thigh angrily. "This sounds so stupid even to me . . . but Marilyn bought this book." Marilyn was Whitney's lover, the latest one. I hadn't met her, but I was almost bound to sooner or later. The Austin lesbian community isn't so large that its various circles don't overlap, even though my set is mostly, shall we say, a bit more mature than Whitney's.

"It's about people who've been abducted by UFOs," she continued. "I never believed any of that stuff before, but she got to reading me parts of it, and I thought of that dream and I just got the feeling right away that that's what that dream is about. I *know* that's it! Otherwise, why would the thought just leap into my mind like that? I can't remember what happened, but I know something did. They *take* little kids that age, you know? I don't know what they do with them, but they keep letting them go and then coming back later and taking them again. They follow them and pick them up every few years. Or that's what the book says, anyway. And I think they did that to me, and I'm terrified.''

"That's a frightening thing to think about," I said. "Since you connected the dream with UFOs, has there been anything else that's come to mind? Any more details about the dream, or any more unexplained memories?''

"No. Well, yeah, but it's . . . it's just a feeling. I feel like there was somebody else there, but I can't see them." She shook her head in frustration. "I can't really explain it," she said. "I just wish I could *remember*."

"When did you first have this dream?''

"Sometime when I was a little kid. It's just always been there.''

I thought the dream was about something pretty deep-seated with Whitney, but I doubted that it could be UFOs, although that was a subject on which I was admittedly uninformed. I suggested we try guided imagery in our next session to open up those memories, and I also suggested she commit the matter to her unconscious self (Whitney not acknowledging any other Higher Power) with the idea of getting to the truth of it in her dreams. She had unusually good dream recall, as a rule.

Whitney agreed, looking noticeably brighter now that the ordeal of telling all this was over.

"And Whitney," I said, looking her firmly in the eye, "you're not crazy.''

She smiled her gratitude. It was a thoroughly charming smile, a fact which was not entirely lost on her therapist.

Chapter 2

My Mustang wouldn't start. Some people would tell me that's what I get for having a classic American car instead of getting a new European or Japanese one every year, but I love the way a '66 Mustang looks—though it didn't look so pretty sitting frustratingly immobile in the parking lot. I trudged back up to the office and called Juno.

"Is it the battery?" She sounded as if she'd been running, huffing and puffing a bit. Probably out in the yard when the phone rang, I thought. It wasn't in her to let the answering machine catch the call.

"I don't think it's the battery. It grinds away when I turn the key, but nothing else happens."

"Hm." She thought about it. "Did you check to see if it's the choke sticking again? You remember that's what it was when this happened before."

I'd forgotten the choke incident entirely. To me, a car is just a way to get from one place to another, albeit, for preference, with a certain style. I feel that as far as the driver is concerned, the engine should always remain decently covered by the hood. "What do I look for?" I asked with resignation.

June told me what to do, a relatively ungreasy operation, she assured me, involving unscrewing something and taking something off and poking open a "butterfly." I now remembered this butterfly from the previous incident months ago as a metal flap that resembled its insect namesake not at all. I kept the sigh out of my voice, thanked

June, said I'd be home soon if I didn't call her right back, and marched out to do battle with the iron beast.

Once I'd heaved the hood up and located what June had told me to look for, the magical ritual of unscrewing and poking and re-screwing worked. The car started as if no other behavior had ever crossed its innocent, mechanical mind.

"I hope it's not going to make a habit of this," I told June later as I scrubbed the smudges of engine dirt from my hands.

She leaned against the frame of the bathroom door watching me, hands in the pockets of her grass-speckled jeans and a grin on her face. I'd been right; she'd been out in the back yard running the weedeater when I'd called. "But you know what to do for it now," she said.

"Oh, please! I have no desire to make like a grease monkey every time I need to start my car. If it does it again, it's going straight to the shop."

"But why spend money when you can fix it yourself?" She feigned wide-eyed innocence. "Don't you like the feeling of self-sufficiency it gives you? That sense of power in the face of adversity?"

"Not as much as I like turning the key and driving off instead of spending twenty minutes groping around in that filthy labyrinth under the hood." I lathered my hands again. "Damn! Doesn't this stuff ever come off?"

"You work on it while I get supper on the table. And it didn't take you twenty minutes. You were home in twenty minutes."

I refused to dignify that with an answer.

We ate supper on the deck overlooking the koi pool. Dusk had taken the sledgehammer quality out of the mid-summer heat, and June, always one for the open air, had set the table before I could suggest the air-conditioned alternative. Not that dining on the deck was really unpleasant, but I'm an indoor girl and like my comforts. I felt I'd been earthy enough already today, considering my mechanical adventure.

"Delicious," I said as I foraged with my spoon among the fruit in my bowl, looking for the strawberries. June's cooking left nothing to be desired. I'd miss it if she followed through on her latest ambition and left me for forestry school. I realized this with a small shock. I'd thought I'd been though all the ramifications of her leaving, and here was another one, and not a minor one, either. This was something I'd be having to deal with every single evening.

I looked across the table and found her watching me. "It's better if you don't try to sort it all out," she said, indicating my fruit compote. "That's why I mixed it up in the first place. The flavors complement each other."

"I like the strawberries alone."

She shrugged. "It's your loss, then." She conveyed a spoonful of mixed fruit to her mouth and ecstatically and ostentatiously closed her eyes as she chewed.

"Did you hear from your school today?" I said, taking the bull by the horns.

"Nope." She said it lightly, but there was a wary look in her eye.

"Maybe tomorrow, then."

"I hope. You wouldn't change your mind and run up there with me for a weekend? It's really pretty country."

I'd refused that invitation when it had first been offered. I hadn't wanted to encourage June in the initial stages of the enterprise, but I was beginning to bow to the inevitable by this time. And at least if I did go, I'd know what her new home was going to be like. I could see June fitting in so well as a forester that I couldn't really hope any longer that she wouldn't go through with it. Graduate school in forestry would suit her down to the ground. I just wished she could get what she wanted here at U.T. instead of two hundred miles away in East Texas. But there were, as she'd patiently pointed out to me, no forests here.

"I'd have to move several appointments if I went," I said.

"Could you do that?"

"I guess so."

June grinned. "I can't wait for you to see what it's like!"

"I'm not moving up there," I said, "so don't get your hopes up about that."

"We'll see." She got up to clear the table, humming happily, and I picked up some dishes and followed her.

The phone rang as I was storing the leftovers in the refrigerator, and I wiped my hands on a cup towel and went to answer it.

"T.D.?" The voice was hesitant. "This is Whitney Way."

Whitney had never called me at home before, though I'd told her she was welcome to if the need arose. It had been three days since the session in which she'd introduced the UFO-dream story. Now, when I asked how she was, she said, "Scared."

"What's scaring you?" I settled into the chair by the phone, raising an eyebrow to June as she went by and mouthing the word, "client." June nodded in reply and vanished into the bedroom.

"God, T.D., it just sounds so stupid! It's this damn UFO stuff. I had that dream again last night, and I realized that there was somebody else definitely there besides me. But I couldn't make myself look to see who it was. Or *what* it was. And now all day long I've had spells where I just get terrified, without any reason, and I just feel like I must be losing my mind."

I suggested that this was probably the memory of whatever had happened working to the surface, that what had happened was in the past, that it was already a fact in her life, not something she had yet to live through.

"You've survived it, whatever it was," I told her.

That made sense to her. I assured her that she could call me any time she needed to, she thanked me, and we hung up.

I sat there thinking. Whitney wasn't the type to panic like this. Whatever this thing was, it was obviously a big one to her. I couldn't even venture a guess yet as to what it might be, but our next session ought to be interesting.

I went into the bedroom to find June, arrayed in her Chinese silk robe with the red and gold dragons, lounging provocatively across the bed. I sat down beside her.

"Shouldn't a forester be wearing something a little more earthy?" I asked, fingering an edge of the material. "Maybe something in a buffalo plaid?"

She looked up at me with eyes that held an unmistakable promise and said, "If this isn't earthy enough for you, I can take it off."

"Oh, yes?"

She stroked the back of my hand lightly with a finger, keeping eye contact. "Or you can."

I willingly followed that suggestion.

Chapter 3

Despite the panic phone call, I half-expected Whitney to have cooled off about the UFO idea by the next time I saw her. It didn't seem like something she'd normally hang onto, although I could see how the combination of the dream and her lover's reading had suggested the idea to her, and certainly such a grotesque possibility would frighten anybody. But Whitney was a down-to-earth type who scoffed, though sometimes rather defensively, at anything which smacked of the spiritual or the supernatural, and I'd not have suspected her of credulousness when it came to extraterrestrial abductions by little green men.

"It wasn't a little green man. I saw him, T.D." I had not, of course, said anything about my stereotypical view of UFO occupants. That came from Whitney's own head, or maybe she'd snatched it from mine. I don't rule out the possibility of ESP; there's too much evidence for it. With some of my clients I almost feel I have to guard my thoughts as well as my visible reactions.

"Tell me about it," I said. Whitney sighed and shifted a little, still relaxed from the session of guided imagery.

Guided imagery is a technique wherein the therapist and client agree to explore a difficult point through a combination of deep relaxation and mental imagery, the therapist guiding the client's visualizations through suggestion. It provides a method for getting at things the client is having difficulty dealing with on a purely conscious level. By agreeing to allow the therapist to guide her, the client is able to circumvent her censors and open herself to ideas or, in this case, memories she might otherwise repress.

Despite the fact that she had a lot of unresolved control issues and so had shown some reluctance to embrace the technique initially, Whitney and I had established in previous stages of her therapy that we could use guided imagery with good success, and she had readily agreed to try it now.

"Hell," she'd said fervently, "I'd just about walk through fire to get to the bottom of this!" She'd shuddered a little. "Well, maybe not walk through *fire*, but I sure do want to get this thing laid to rest."

"You can do that," I'd told her.

She'd looked at me with more hope than belief, then said, rather grimly, "Let's do it."

"Sit back, get completely comfortable, and close your eyes," I began. My voice was slow, calm, soothing. "Now breathe deeply . . . inhale, and as you inhale, you draw in energy into every part of your body. Exhale . . . You breathe out tension. You feel the tension flowing out. You let it go. Let go of the tension in your feet. Your feet feel heavy, relaxed . . . your legs, your hands . . . your arms feel heavy . . ." Whitney, used to the process, relaxed visibly, letting her head fall back against the back of the couch, her hands going slack in her lap. I took her through the major muscle groups, relaxing each in turn. It was interesting to see her face, usually very mobile and expressive, smooth into the baby-like blankness of sleep.

But guided imagery is not a kind of sleep. It's a physically inactive state, but a very mentally active one, in which the subject is free to explore her inner world. The therapist's suggestions are only suggestions, not commands, and the client can follow them or not, as she wills.

Whitney was a good subject. When she was relaxed and breathing easily, we took her back to the scene of the dream. "You are in the forest," I told her, "behind the pine tree, but this time you aren't afraid. You see something, a light, and you hear a sound. You can look around the tree and see where the light and the sound are coming from.''

I saw her breathing rhythm change a little, her face muscles twitch.

"You're very relaxed,'' I said, reassuring her, "not afraid. Nothing can hurt you. What you see is a memory. You've lived through it, and you're okay. All you're doing now is remembering something you saw a long time ago.'' Her breathing deepened a little, slowed.

"You look around the pine tree, and you can see what's causing the light and the sound. If there's anybody there, you can talk to them. You may ask them what they're doing . . . .'' I waited a moment. "You can talk to whoever is there . . . . You're not afraid. You tell whoever is there that you're not afraid, that you've lived many more years and that whatever they're doing hasn't hurt you. You tell them to stop frightening you now . . . .''

I waited until Whitney had had time to visualize all that. Then, "When you're ready, you can leave,'' I continued. "When you finish talking to whoever's there, you turn and walk away. Nobody can come after you or hurt you. You're not afraid. You walk away through the forest.'' I waited a moment more, then said, "When you want to, you can open your eyes.'' After a moment she sighed, and her eyes fluttered open. That was when she said that about its not being a little green man she'd seen.

"It was some kind of a man, I think, but he didn't seem real, or like a real human being. He was doing something with his hands, and the light was coming from there, from his hands. It was just like a huge, blinding light, growing and growing until I couldn't see anything else at all. And, T.D., it was the *light* that made the sound!''

"Did you talk to him?''

"No.'' She frowned. "I knew if he saw me, I'd be dead.''

"Would he have killed you?''

"I don't know. I just knew I'd be dead.'' She shook herself and grinned, masking the seriousness of her concern. "Some dream, huh?''

"A scary one. What did the man look like?"

"He had on some kind of shiny clothes, kind of silvery, only they seemed to have different colors in them, yellow and orange, that seemed to shift and change. I have the impression they were made out of something that reflected light."

"How about his face? Did you get a good look at it?"

"I didn't pay any attention to his face, because all I was looking at was his hands, what he was doing. But I couldn't really see that because of the light. I just know it terrified me, whatever it was."

I thought a minute. "What else was there? Did you see anything, any kind of object?" I couldn't quite bring myself to say, "space ship."

She shook her head.

"How did the man get there?"

Whitney frowned. "I don't know . . . . It *seems* like there was something else there, but . . . ." She thought a minute, then shrugged. "I don't know. All I could see was the light." She paused, wrestling with something. "No, I can't get it. There was something else there, all right, but I have the feeling it was just too awful to think about."

With this information we had to be content, at least for the time being. I asked her to continue to commit the matter to her unconscious self and to record her dreams, with the idea that the memories might come up in that form. "They'll come when they're ready," I told her.

"Well, *I'm* ready," she said.

"Good," I said. I, too, was curious.

Chapter 4

"Congratulations!" I laid the acceptance letter back on the table between us and smiled at my beaming friend. "So, you're going to be a forester."

"It looks like it," June said. Her high color and sparkling eyes belied the casual tone.

I opened the refrigerator and put ice cubes in a glass. "This calls for a celebration," I said, trying to put genuine warmth in my voice despite the cold in the pit of my stomach. "Would you like a drink?"

"Yes, please." Then, "Oh, T.D., I can't believe it! I've been accepted! I've been accepted!" And she leapt across the space between us and hugged me, spinning us around in a wild, whirling dance while I held a glass of ice awkwardly behind her back.

"Here, let me fix the drinks," I said when we'd come to a stop. Who could begrudge a friend such happiness? June rescued the chair we'd half knocked over, and I set whiskey sours on the coffee table while she selected a tape and flipped on the stereo.

"I haven't even thought about dinner," she said, settling into a corner of the couch. "I was just too excited. What do you think about going out?"

"Great. And it's my treat, my girl. This is your night."

"If it's my night, you know what I'd really like to do?" she said in a voice full of youthful eagerness. June, at twenty-nine, is five years younger than I am.

"What would you like to do?" I said, matching her enthusiasm with my tone.

"I'd like to go dancing!" The smile stayed on her face, but the question was there, too: Could she persuade her stodgy friend to brave the public dance floor at a lesbian bar?

I almost never went to the bar if I could avoid it. For one thing, I'm not much of a drinker. For another, alas, I'm not much of a dancer. June had tried to convince me for three years that we danced as well as most of the couples there and that nobody was watching us, anyway. She might have been right about how well we danced, comparatively speaking, but she was wrong about our not being watched. Clients of mine would inevitably be there, many of them consumed with curiosity about my private life. We would certainly be watched.

Several years ago, the first time this argument had come up, I'd tried to explain my reluctance to June.

"It's like you used to feel about your school teachers," I had begun. "Didn't you seize eagerly on any little tidbit about their lives outside the classroom?"

"Just the ones I had crushes on."

I had tried to go on to explain some of the ramifications of the client-therapist relationship, but June, who had neither been in therapy herself nor apparently ever talked to anyone who had, had interrupted me with, "Good god, you mean all these fucked-up women you see go around dreaming of getting you into bed? Christ, *that* makes me feel secure!"

"Transference is just a part of the therapeutic process," I had said, starting to defend my clients, the reference to whom as "fucked-up" I found I resented. "It certainly isn't always sexual. Sometimes the therapist becomes the focus of a client's anger, or —"

"I know I sure as hell wanted to get to bed with Miss Cosgrove in junior high!" she exclaimed, referring to a teacher on whom she had had a notorious crush. Obviously my reference to teachers and their students had been an unfortunate choice of example. And June had refused, after that, to listen to any further explanations. "Don't pull all that more-rational-than-thou, high and mighty therapist bullshit on me!" she had finally shouted. "I don't notice your being so cool and collected when you're on your back!"

This had not been June at her best, but that had been very early in our relationship. We had dealt with those issues more rationally since then.

Now I smiled and gave her a peck on the cheek. "I'd love to go dancing with you," I said. The joyous hug I got made me glad I'd said it.

That was how June and I found ourselves, after a sumptuous Greek dinner, installed at a little round table with a good view of the raised wooden dance floor at Petticoat Junction, with country music blaring and women in cowboy clothes two-stepping stylishly (or awkwardly —I had to admit style wasn't present in every case) before us in a circling parade.

Certainly it was a colorful spectacle, and there was a degree of comfort here that I wouldn't have found in many places, the ease of being a member of the majority group. It would be the men and the heterosexuals who would be out of place here.

June, of course, was in her element. She'd switched to beer after dinner and had worn her roper boots. I don't own any western clothes, so I was still in what June derogatorily referred to as "therapist drag," loose cotton slacks in blue and a big, roughly-woven shirt in pale yellow, and instead of boots I sported my Reeboks. But I was getting into the spirit of the thing, just the same, and June and I two-stepped several songs with the best of them. In the mirror at one side of the dance floor I watched us each time we passed in the throng, June taller than me by nearly a head, broad-shouldered and straight-backed, her booted feet moving lightly and stylishly to the music, and myself looking small, almost delicate in her arms. Whirling spots of reflected light crossed my shoulders, the frothy red halo of my hair, and June's freckled face and short, brown locks, gliding over our arms and dappling us with otherworldly effect.

We were doing a slow country waltz, my head against June's shoulder, when one member of a passing couple reached out and tapped me and smiled and waved. It was Caroline, an acquaintance from before I met June, when I used to socialize more widely than I now did. After the song was finished and June and I were back at our table, she and the woman with her stopped to say hello.

She opened the conversation with, "T.D., I thought you'd died!"

"It has been a while, Caroline. Have you met June?"

They shook hands and Caroline introduced her friend Roya ("Like 'Royal,' but without the *l*," she smiled. "Or like 'Roy' with an *a*."), and they pulled chairs from a neighboring table and sat down with us. I'd always found Caroline unexpectedly interesting to talk to—one of those people who manage to seem dull *in absentia* but delightful in person —but the bar is not the best place to talk. It was getting late and it was a weeknight, so after a few minutes, when Roya suggested going out for coffee together, June and I agreed.

There was a short wait at Kirby Lane South for a table in the smoking section because Roya smoked ("If it won't bother anybody?" she'd said in such a way that we knew she meant it). We gave our orders to the young, semi-bearded waiter and then looked at each other in one of those pauses that so often come before someone opens a social conversation with relative strangers. Caroline looked thinner and at the same time more sinewy than I'd remembered, as if she'd been going regularly to the gym, but it was Roya who took my eye.

Roya was a very attractive woman. She, like Caroline, was thin, but there was not a trace of that angular awkwardness I often associate with thin women. Her fingers were long and tapered, and I found myself, when I could tear my eyes away from her open smile and the lights in her eyes, watching her fascinating hands as she smoked her Benson and Hedges. She wore a labyris pinky ring, and that reminded me of my client Whitney Way, who wore a similar one, but on the opposite hand. Then I felt June watching me, and I shook myself out of my momentary trance and said the first thing that came into my mind: "Does anybody here know anything about UFOs?"

This startling opening was well-received. Yes, Caroline had read several fascinating books about The Phenomenon, as she called it in obvious capitals, and I set out to inform myself secondhand about the thing that was frightening Whitney. June, too, to my surprise, had read fairly extensively on the subject at one time, so she and Caroline energetically shared their knowledge while I listened and injected the occasional pertinent question.

UFO contactees, it seemed, often reported memory lapses. UFOs sometimes made loud humming or roaring sounds. Another thing associated with them was brilliant light, which, when it struck the hapless witness, often caused a kind of temporary paralysis. Whitney's dream, practically to the letter.

While I was fishing out the information I wanted, Roya simply listened—except that there was nothing simple about it. She listened with animation and energy, her eyes darting from one speaker to the other, her sensitive face registering a panoply of emotions as the tales unfolded. I longed to hear her talk, to see what kind of ideas she had, but this wasn't her subject, obviously. Too bad I'd chosen this instead of something Roya knew better.

"I liked your friend Caroline," June said in the car later. "We ought to get together with them sometime."

"Yes, let's. It was nice being with different people for a change."

"And you could probably stand having Roya around, too," she said with a sly, sideways look.

"I thought Roya was quite attractive," I said with dignity.

"No shit?" said my irreverent friend. "Who'd ever have guessed it?"

Altogether it had been a satisfying evening, and the reason for the celebration, June's acceptance at graduate school far away, had for the most part obediently remained out of my consciousness. Drifting toward sleep, listening to June's soft, regular breathing, I thought briefly of that and pushed it back again.

Images of the evening's experiences glided across my relaxing mind: the dancing couples, the smooth fabric of June's western shirt against my cheek, the whiskery waiter at Kirby Lane, Roya's dark, delightsome eye catching mine, the humming, brightly-lit (and, I couldn't help thinking, probably fictional) alien craft and their paralyzed victims.

It did sound ominously like Whitney's dream. It all seemed to fit, so well that I wondered if Whitney might have read these things and forgotten she'd read them. I wondered what these images might symbolize to her. Then, just as sleep closed down thought, one fleeting, disturbing idea crossed my mind: I heard again Whitney's voice saying, "I knew if he saw me, I'd be dead." I'd questioned my two informers closely on that point and the consensus was unshakable: UFOs didn't kill people.

Whitney's dream—or memory—was going to require deeper investigation.

Chapter 5

As it turned out, Whitney herself was investigating her dream symbols, and the things she was turning up were startling.

"There was a dead body, T.D." She said it flatly, unquestioningly, the way she might have said, "It's hot outside," or "I like home-grown tomatoes."

"Did you dream of a dead body?"

She frowned. "I guess I did. I just woke up yesterday morning realizing that the UFO man was standing over a dead body. I guess I dreamed it. All I know is, I remember it."

"Can you describe this body?" A dead body could mean any number of things in Whitney's personal symbology; by encouraging her to talk about the details of the symbol itself, I hoped to uncover some possibilities of its meaning.

Whitney's frown deepened, and she closed her eyes in concentration, pinching her brows together with her left hand. It was a habit of hers, obviously her way of conveying to me that she was deep in thought. I waited, watching her silver labyris pinky ring gleaming like Roya's had done last night at Kirby Lane. What a thoroughly fascinating woman! We'd certainly have them over for drinks soon.

"I just have a general impression," Whitney said, looking up.

"Which is . . . ?"

"Well, the UFO guy—God, it sounds so stupid to keep calling him that! But anyway, the guy there is standing over a body lying on the ground." She held my eyes with hers, trying to read my reaction. When I didn't respond at once, she shrugged helplessly and said, "Really, that's all I remember."

I suggested we try guided imagery again in light of this new memory, in hopes that the light trance state would facilitate the recovery of more detail. But although Whitney agreed readily, the experiment failed to yield much more than we already had. Except for one thing, that is, and this I disregarded at the time.

"For some reason I keep thinking how dry everything is," she told me. "I know it must have been in the summer, because it was so hot. But why would a little kid keep thinking of how dry the weather has been?"

"People often talk about the weather to avoid talking about more personal things," I suggested.

"So maybe I'm just trying to distract myself from what's really there?"

I waited.

"Maybe the memory is so awful that I'm even talking to *myself* about the weather? 'Hi, Whitney! Hot enough for ya? Sure could use some rain. Yep, sure could. Never seen it so dry in June before.' Hell, T.D.! Just hell." She hit her thigh three deliberate blows with her fist.

"You're very frustrated by this."

"Goddamned right I'm frustrated! I've got something I'm trying to keep hidden from myself, and it's my *own* experience! A part of my own life! Dammit, I have a right to know what happened to me! I mean, it happened to me!"

"The memories seem to be coming back little by little," I said. "They're not quite ready, but they'll come when they are."

"Well, it's taking too damn long. I want to get on with my life." She smiled wryly at me. "It's not like I don't have anything else to work on here."

I smiled back.

"And Marilyn's parents are coming this weekend."

We spent the rest of the session on that impending crisis.

Chapter 6

I had a crisis of my own when I got home that evening. It started, as I thought, innocently enough. June was poring over the catalog of the Stephen F. Austin State University School of Forestry. This seemed to be her major activity since she'd received her acceptance letter, and I thought she ought to take a break from hypothetical course selection and do something a little more sociable for a change. I was bored.

"What did you have in mind?" she asked, marking her place with a fingertip.

"Well, we could run out to the mall and look for those shoes I wanted." I needed some yellow shoes to match a nice shirt I'd picked up on sale.

"Um." Her enthusiasm was overwhelming. I saw her eyes stray back to the catalog entry.

"Or if that doesn't inspire you, we could rent a movie. It's been a while since we did that. I know! We could see if we can get something Caroline and Roya would like and ask them over."

"I guess we could. It's kind of short notice."

"We can ask." I got my address book out of my purse and went to the phone. "What would you like to see?" I asked over my shoulder as I dialed.

June, however, didn't reply. She'd gone back to her catalog. I felt a little peeved, but I turned my attention to the phone.

Caroline answered. I felt a slight prick of disappointment that it hadn't been Roya. I put my proposition to her, but she declined the invitation. They were both tired from their rowing lesson and just wanted to stay home.

"Your rowing lesson?"

"Yes. We went down to Town Lake and took a lesson, and it's fabulous! It's exhausting, though. But I understand it gets easier."

"What did you row? Not one of those thin little shells?" I'd seen them on the lake, and they looked impossibly precarious to me.

That was indeed what they'd rowed, and Caroline waxed practically poetic about the wonders of whole-body exercise, a subject which interested me not at all. I am, as I may have mentioned, an indoor type, and I try to confine my athletics to attending Lady Longhorns games and watching the Astros on television when I can't get out of it. I finally got Caroline off the phone and broke into June's study of her eternal catalog to tell her about my conversation.

"Just as well," she said. "I really don't feel much like a movie, anyway."

"Then why didn't you say that before I called them?"

"I did."

"No, you didn't."

"I did, but let's not argue about it. Anyway, I've just about decided what I want to take," she said, referring to the catalog. "The first semester—"

"Spare me!" I cried in an unguarded moment of candor. She looked surprised, and then her expression changed to one of mulish displeasure. I back-pedaled a little. "I'd love to hear about your plans, but right now we need to decide what we're going to do tonight. Then you can tell me all about it."

June was not appeased. "Okay, T.D.," she said, closing the catalog and stacking it and her notes together with exaggerated patience, "tell me what you want us to do tonight."

"It's not just what I want us to do," I began in a reasonable tone. "I just thought you and I could spend a little time together for a change and do something fun, something we'd both enjoy. I've hardly seen you since you got that damned acceptance letter." The "damned" just slipped in. June opened her mouth, and I went on hastily, "And I miss you, honey."

That was true, I realized. I did miss June, although we'd been together as much lately as we usually were. I knew, of course, that the problem was that we were both anticipating June's leaving in the fall, and that was affecting our relationship. "Let's not withdraw from each other like this," I went on. "We both feel anxious about your leaving, but let's not let it spoil the time we have left."

"Huh?" Either she hadn't followed my analysis or June felt like misunderstanding. "What do you mean? I don't feel anxious about my leaving. I'm excited about my leaving. Maybe *you* feel anxious. *I* feel excited."

I held myself in and said, "When you spend all your time studying your catalog, I feel ignored, and I want you to take a little time away from that to be with me so we can share some of the other things in our lives."

"Oh, is that what you want? Okay, we can do that." I started to smile, but she went on, "But it seems to me that you could be a little enthusiastic about my school. After all, it's the chance for me to make something of myself, to do what I really want to do for a change. God knows I'm sick of hanging around here trying to get a kick out of going to work in that stuffy office and coming home and watching rented movies on the VCR with people I can't even talk to without being psychoanalyzed. Christ, T.D., don't you get sick of it, too?"

"Nobody's psychoanalyzing anybody. I'm just saying that's it's perfectly normal for us to feel somewhat off balance when we know a big change is coming up, and—"

"There! You're doing it without even knowing it!"

"I see you're very angry."

"Yes!" June slapped the table and stood up. "I'm angry! I'm angry about just being another client to you! Why can't you ever just come out and say what you feel? Say you're scared about losing me, or whatever it is. Say keeping me with you is more important to you than my education. Say you're going to make me pay for wanting something you can't give me by making sure I see how boring you find the whole thing. At least be honest for once in your life! 'I see you're angry!' Hell, yes! You *make* me angry! Being treated this way would make anybody angry!"

"You can choose to be angry about it, or you can—"

"I don't *choose* to be angry! I said you *make* me angry. Listen to what I'm saying, will you?"

"When you say I make you angry, that's blaming me for your emotional reaction. I'm willing to take responsibility for my emotions, and I'd hope—"

"Oh, hell!" June turned on her heel and stalked outside, whipping the patio door closed with such force that it bounced back six inches.

I was standing irresolute, debating whether to follow or not, when the phone rang. It was Whitney Way.

"I hate to bother you at home," she said, "but there's going to be a T.V. special on UFOs tonight, and I thought you might catch it, if you're interested." I thanked her, hearing the tension of the argument with June still sounding annoyingly in my voice, and said I'd try to watch it. I didn't have anything better to do. Maybe June would like to see it, too, since it was a subject she was interested in.

June, however, was not ready to bury the hatchet yet. "Not right now," she said when I told her about the show, and she went on hacking at a flower bed with a hoe by the inadequate light of the outdoor floods. I hoped she didn't destroy any plants she didn't mean to; that would offset the tranquilizing effect of the exercise. I turned on the television and slipped a blank tape into the VCR. June could watch the thing later, if it was any good.

The show wasn't so much about UFOs as about people who claimed to be UFO contactees. I expected crackpots and publicity seekers, but these seemed like very ordinary types. They were members of a UFO contactee support group, and the brief explanation of the group and how it operated sounded genuine. The reporter doing the interviews asked leading questions and tried to shake their stories, but the three people featured would not be led or shaken. It was apparent to me that they, at least, believed that what they claimed had happened to them had really happened, or else they had their stories down pat. If what they claimed was true, it was quite frightening. I could imagine that watching this wasn't doing much toward setting Whitney's mind at ease.

Especially unsettling was one of the cases, that of a man who, having had his original experience in his early twenties, now claimed to have been revisited by his UFO contacts several times a year since then. Now in his thirties, he looked haggard and drawn. His hands shook visibly, and his eyes darted about as if always looking for watchers in the shadows. He told a horrifying story about the deterioration of his health, an apparent premature aging which confounded diagnosis.

At first glance he didn't look nearly so credible as the other two witnesses, but the more I watched him, the more I became convinced that he was telling the truth, and his claims were bolstered by information introduced by the interviewer to the effect that several contactees, including some members of this same support group, had experienced similar health problems. One, at least, had died of unexplained causes; two, tragically, had committed suicide.

June wandered in when the hour was half over, stood behind the couch and watched in silence for a few minutes, then went toward the bedroom. I thought she was going to wash up and rejoin me, but she never reappeared. I waited as long as I could, but my attention wasn't on the television. I went to find her.

We were able to talk then. It took a long time, but by the time we went to bed, we were at peace. June had acknowledged her fears about our parting, I had acknowledged mine, and I had agreed to go with her to visit the campus in two weeks. June would take Friday off; we'd stay three days and come back Sunday evening. I'd move or cancel all my appointments for those days, and we'd just have a good time with each other. June would talk to her advisor and look for a place to live in the fall, and I'd get to see the piney woods.

"And we'll have two nights in the motel," June concluded.

Two nights away from home, away from my work and hers, on neutral territory, where maybe we could forget our fears and our differences and relax together the way we had when we were first lovers.

That seemed like the best part of all.

Chapter 7

The motel was panelled in dark knotty pine and smelled faintly of Lysol, but the room was spacious and the bed was firm and inviting. I heaved aside the suitcase June had deposited there and fell back across the quilted spread, arms outflung. "Wonderful!" I cried, throwing my head back and closing my eyes. "I thought I was absolutely molded to the shape of that car seat!"

June, hanging the suit bag in the closet, said, "I told you we should have taken my car."

"You'd have wanted the top down."

"I wanted the top down on yours, too, but you won. So what difference would it have made if we'd taken mine which, you'll have to admit, is a tad more comfortable?"

"Ownership of the vehicle gives one a certain advantage." I was feeling prickly because I was tired and also because I knew she was right: her year-old Le Baron was more comfortable than my Mustang, if only because the seats were newer. We were both paying for my fit of obstinacy.

June turned around and gave me an exasperated look. "Ownership of the vehicle also implies some sort of obligation to one's passenger's comfort, doesn't it? I'd have been happy to have the top up on my car, seeing as how you feel so strongly about not being exposed to the elements."

"Thank you for your consideration."

June sighed and went into the bathroom, closing the door behind her. It had been a long trip.

The bedspread felt cool against my weary back. I'd overheated just lugging in the luggage. Whitney, when last we'd talked, had been half right about the climate in East Texas, and I told June about it when she came out of the bathroom, unwrapping the paper from a plastic motel glass. "It's supposed to be cool under the pines and in the valleys and hot everywhere else. The heat, at least, is living up to its press," I said.

Whitney, when I had told her last week that I was going to be out of town for a few days, had laughed and said, "Good!"

I was somewhat taken aback. "Good?" I had echoed. It was not the usual client's reaction to a cancellation.

"Good," she had repeated. "I think you need a vacation, T.D. A person can get stressed out working with us crazy people all the time," she had gone on, deliberately pushing one of my buttons. My clients have problems, but they're certainly not crazy. She had grinned as I opened my mouth to protest, and had rushed on. "You need time to heal, to get in touch with your feelings," she had teased. Then she had relented and explained. "I was going to tell you I wouldn't be here next week, either. They're having a family get-together back home, and I'm going up there."

"Back to East Texas?"

"Home to the piney woods hills," she had affirmed. "I haven't been up there in a coon's age, and it'll be nice to see some of my cousins I've lost touch with. Also, I thought I'd talk to my sister and see if she can maybe remember something that would shed some light on my lovely dream of death and terror."

She had spoken lightly, but her eyes had told another story. "So where are you going?" she had asked, turning the conversation away from that topic.

When I had told her, she had said, "No kidding? That's not but about twenty miles from where I'm going! We're from Redland, and Stephen F. Austin's right over in Nacogdoches." Then she had gone on to describe the countryside in glowing terms.

Now, a week later and gratefully installed in the Pine Bough Motel in Nacogdoches, I lay across the welcoming bed and mused upon what Whitney had said. The pines, tall and somber and resinous, were a nice change from the live oaks of Austin, and I supposed she'd been telling the truth about the coolness to be found in their shade, though I wasn't planning to venture into the outdoors to find out. Certainly she'd been right about the heat. It had been a dry spring, followed by a hot, rainless summer. The red dust was over everything, as if the landscape was a long-disused room in need of the housekeeper's attention, and the Forest Service billboards from which Smokey the Bear warned that "Only YOU can prevent forest fires" seemed to lose credibility as one drove through miles and miles of baking vegetation. It looked to me as if only God could prevent the whole world's going up like a tinderbox from spontaneous combustion.

The last thing I wanted to do was go out, now that I was safely in, but, as June patiently pointed out, I'd come to see where she'd be in the fall, and I might as well go through with it. I dragged my weary carcass off the bed and we sallied forth to find the School of Forestry.

The campus was pretty. I had to admit that. The tall, straight trunks of the pines lent a sylvan air to the place that set it in striking contrast to the U.T. campus back in Austin. This one was much smaller, of course, but still of a respectable size, not the small town atmosphere I'd expected.

"Small world," said a voice behind us, directly contradicting my thought. "Fancy meeting you here, T.D.!"

June and I stopped and turned around, waiting while the hurrying figure caught up with us. "June," I said, "this is Whitney Way. Whitney, June Leland. What brings you here? I thought you were at your family reunion."

"Was." Whitney was panting a little from her dash to overtake us. "But . . . ." She hesitated, looking suddenly shy and covering it with a grin. "How could I pass up seeing my therapist for a whole week?"

"How, indeed?" I saw June looking surreptitiously at her watch while keeping a pleasant and mildly interested expression on her face. Her appointment with her advisor was in about five minutes, and we hadn't even found the Forestry Department yet. I saw that Whitney had something on her mind that wasn't going to come out with the three of us standing there in the middle of the sidewalk, and it must be pretty nearly of crisis proportions to have brought her here looking for me, if in fact it had. June was sensitive enough to see that as soon as I did, and she said, "T.D., why don't I meet you back at the motel about five? I've got to run right now if I'm not going to be late."

"All right," I said, looking at her to see if it was really all right for me to abandon her. From the abstracted look in her eyes, I saw it was. It was a look I'd seen there a lot lately, and now it struck me that I was seeing it through the faint images of the campus pine trees reflected in her glasses. Suddenly it seemed to me that those images had somehow been there even back in Austin. I thought, When she's thinking about her forestry, she isn't seeing me at all. A small knot tightened somewhere in my chest.

"See you later, then," June was saying. "Nice to meet you, Whitney." She smiled cordially now that she knew we weren't going to delay her further and half-raised a hand in farewell, already turning to go. I watched her stride away, her arms swinging and her long, slim legs thrusting her quickly on toward her appointment with the future.

When I turned to face Whitney again, she was watching me curiously. "June's the friend who's going to school up here?" she asked.

I broke away from my own thoughts and smiled at my client. "Yes. And now, what brings you here?" I said, fleeing into therapist mode.

"Let's get some coffee somewhere. It's a long story."

It was an intriguing one, as well. Over the plastic-topped table in the Dairy Queen, Whitney, her brows knit in a worried frown, poured it all out.

"I didn't know where to start at first, about trying to find out about that dream, you know, so I just dived in and asked if anybody had ever seen a UFO."

"Who did you ask?"

"There were a bunch of cousins and all, sitting around, the way we always do at these family things. The older people stay downstairs, the women in the dining room mostly and the men in the living room or out on the porch, where they can smoke. I guess they could smoke in the house now that my grandma's dead, but that's how it got started, anyway. They had to go outside and smoke on the porch because she didn't like for them to smoke in the house, so they still do. And we all gather upstairs, all of us of my generation. Sprawl on the beds and all. It's what we've done since we were kids."

"And had they?"

"Huh? Oh, had they seen a UFO? Yeah! They had! My cousin Connie had, anyway, and Jo Ann and Margie remembered about it, too. They hadn't seen it, but they all knew about it, all the ones that were just a little older than me."

I waited expectantly.

"It seems this was all a big UFO flap area about the time I was five or six. I couldn't pin anybody down on the year exactly, but I know how I can."

"And how is that?"

"Easy. It was also a year we had a bad drought." She pronounced it to rhyme with "south." I'd pronounced it that way, too, growing up in West Texas, but the broadcast news pronunciation had convinced me I was hopelessly provincial in that. I was interested to hear that the East Texas version coincided with my own.

"I remember you said there was something in your dream about how dry it was," I said.

"Yeah. Well, they remembered that there was a lot of talk about the flying saucers being involved in starting the big forest fire that nearly burned up Redland that year. And Connie, the one who saw one of them, said it was a bright light in the sky just at twilight, and it was kind of swaying in place over the woods that burned later. A lot of people saw it, and then when the fire happened, they talked about maybe that had something to do with starting it."

"So, you think you could ferret out more information about that time by finding out when the fire was? By searching through the morgue at the newspaper office, maybe?"

"Better than that. I asked my Uncle—he works for the Forest Service at Lufkin—and he said he didn't remember, but I think he just didn't want to talk to me. He's not the most talkative man I know. I remember I was always a little scared of him when I was a kid."

"What made you afraid of him?"

"Oh, I guess it was just that he never seemed like he liked kids much. Most everybody else in the family did. Anyway, there's a guy up here in the forestry department who would know all about the fire, because he directed the firefighting and nearly got burned to death. His name's Ross Barnett. My sister remembered him coming to the house with my uncle when we were little. I came over to hunt him up and see what he remembers. If I can find out the year, then I can go to the newspapers and look up UFO reports from then."

"You don't think your older relatives would remember?" I was wondering why she hadn't just asked around more in her family.

"Well ..." Whitney paused to sip her iced tea. I watched her. "It's ... well, it's just that I don't feel really comfortable talking about it. I mean, I know they'd laugh at me, you know?"

"And it's important that they take you seriously."

"Yeah. Yeah, I guess it is. I don't have the right credentials to be taken seriously by my family. No husband, no kids —well, you know. They think I'm just playing around, not getting down to the real business of living."

"The real business of living is getting married and having children?"

"Yeah, they think so. They wonder if I'll ever grow

up. So I don't really feel like talking up this UFO business which they're going to think is just kiddie stuff."

"Fantasy."

"Tall stories, yeah."

"And Ross Whoever—"

"Barnett."

"—Ross Barnett will take it seriously?"

"Hey, I'm not going to mention flying saucers to him! All I'm going to ask about is the year of the big Redland fire. He's got to take that seriously; he nearly died in it."

"Yes, that's serious, all right."

"And maybe I can get him to tell me if they ever found out what started it. But I'll bet, whether they know or not, they'll say it was lightning or a trash fire or a careless camper or something. Still, it never hurts to ask, does it?"

"No, it doesn't hurt to ask."

Three college-age boys had come into the Dairy Queen and were boisterously discussing the prospects of the fall football season for the Stephen F. Austin Lumberjacks. When they sat at the table next to us and started looking our way and grinning, Whitney and I smiled at each other and simultaneously said, "Shall we go now?" We both laughed at the mutual reaction and, dropping our paper cups into the trash receptacle, we walked into the heat of the outdoors again.

Out on the sidewalk, I said, "So now you're off to find your forester?"

"I guess so. I'm a little nervous. I get nervous about this whole thing, every time I think about it. It was good to run into you, T.D."

"Yes," I agreed. "I'm very interested in what you're finding out." We came to the intersection where Whitney would have to cross the street to head back to campus and I'd go the other way to the motel, and there we stopped for a moment. "I guess I'll walk back to the motel and wait for my own forester," I said. I didn't want Whitney to feel I was being secretive and closety about my relationship with June, since it was so obvious, anyway.

"June is studying forestry?" she asked with interest.

"She will be this fall. I'm going to miss her."

Whitney looked at me speculatively but didn't pursue that farther. "Didn't she say she'd meet you there at five?" she asked. "There's plenty of time; why don't you come along with me?"

Why not, indeed? I had nothing to do at the motel but read, and I would like to see the forestry department, after all. "Let's go!" I said, and was rewarded with Whitney's openly delighted smile.

Chapter 8

Ross Barnett wasn't in his office, but the department secretary, a friendly young woman with a collection of large and flashy rings on her fingers, suggested that we might find him at home and, when she discovered we were from out of town, went so far as to look up his number and call him herself.

"Professor Barnett?" she said into the receiver while smiling at me and Whitney, "There are two visitors here who'd like to talk to you . . . . I don't know. Just a minute." She held out the phone to me, and I gestured toward Whitney, who took it.

Whitney identified herself by name and continued, "I'm Jimmy Cowley's niece, from Redland." This information was apparently well received, because she went on at some length about the health of her uncle and his wife and other such matters, while I occupied myself in contemplating the large oil painting of a pine forest scene which dominated the decor of the office. It was quite well done, I thought, and gave the feeling of coolness and peace which Whitney had so lovingly described to me back in Austin. Maybe June and I could get out into the woods for a little while before we had to go home. It had been a long time since I'd felt inclined toward a nature walk, so I might as well take advantage of the urge. It would, I mused, be a romantic thing to do with my lover, and a little romance would certainly be in order for us right now. We'd been entirely too much at odds lately.

I heard Whitney saying, "I'd be very grateful if I could!" into the phone, and I turned to see her reaching for the piece of paper and the pen being proffered by the secretary. She began scribbling down directions of some kind and repeating them as she wrote. It looked as if she was going to visit the professor at home. I glanced at my watch. Early yet. If she wanted me along, I thought I wouldn't mind the jaunt.

And in fact she had been invited and she did want me. "I'm so excited, T.D.!" she said on the way to where she'd left her car. "I forget how easy it is to deal with people like this."

"People like what?"

"Oh, you know. Home people. People who know my family. It's just so natural. I say who I am and Professor Barnett knows my folks, and I'm welcome to come right out to his house. I didn't even have to go into what I wanted to know from him. People are just so friendly!"

"You don't think people in Austin would treat you this well?"

"Not really. I guess, if they knew me . . . . Hell, I guess what I'm liking so much up here is the feeling of fitting in. Being somebody normal. Part of the whole society."

"Not being so queer?"

Whitney stared ahead, thinking about it, then nodded. "Yeah. Yeah, I guess that's exactly it. I like not automatically being the green monkey."

"What makes the difference, Whitney?"

"Mostly how I feel, I guess. I suppose I don't find myself asking strangers for favors much, anyway." She grinned at me. "So I guess it's really only how I feel, huh?"

"Have you asked any strangers in Austin for favors?" I said, driving home the point.

"No. Well, other people in the community . . . ." (By this I, of course, understood her to mean the lesbian community.) "Not any straight people, though." She paused, thinking about it. "I guess this is my old homophobia acting up again, isn't it?"

I smiled. "It's all in what you tell yourself to pay attention to. I'm not saying the prejudice isn't there, but you might ask yourself how valuable it is to you to focus on it."

"Not very. It's really pretty negative to do that. You're right, T.D."

I nodded.

Whitney looked at me. "But I'm not going to stick my head in the sand, either," she said defiantly.

Good, I thought. It's okay to be realistic about how things are, but not to make ourselves sick over them. I felt gratified by Whitney's self-observation. This was a little breakthrough for her.

Professor Barnett lived in a rather rambling red brick house tucked into a grove of tall pines which dwarfed it. The smooth lawns delicately laced with shade from the deep green branches high overhead were further graced by scattered clumps of white-leaved caladiums, and in a sunny planter box across the front of the porch some kind of yellow and orange flowers blossomed in dazzling profusion. June would have known what they were, but to me they were just a pretty splash of color. I couldn't help thinking I preferred my more aesthetically pure way of seeing them.

We climbed out of Whitney's car and crunched across the gravel driveway to the front walk. Whitney took the lead, stopped at the broad front door with its brass pine cone knocker, searched for a doorbell button, found it, and rang. Footsteps inside announced the arrival of our host, and the door swung open to reveal Professor Ross Barnett.

If June in her Chinese robe had looked an unlikely forester, Ross Barnett made up for it. Faded jeans, lace-up boots, and a much-washed T-shirt with the Stephen F. Austin Lumberjacks logo looked like what Paul Bunyan would have worn if he'd worked in the East Texas summer heat. Ross's well-tanned face and arms and his wide-shouldered muscularity bespoke a man of action, and the

blue eyes looking out from under a stray lock of sandy
hair sparkled. He smiled, showing perfect white teeth.

"Hello, there! Did I just talk to one of you on the
phone?"

I said, "Yes, you talked to Whitney," and Whitney
nodded.

"I'm Ross Barnett," he said, vigorously shaking hands
first with Whitney and then with me as we introduced
ourselves. I watched Ross smile in acknowledgment while
his eyes scanned each of us quickly and comprehensively.
Bachelor? Ladies' man? Whatever, he was certainly aware
of our gender and making that awareness abundantly clear.
I wondered what June's reaction to him might be, and his
to her. Flirtatious glances are only fun if they're noticed,
and June often just doesn't notice men at all, but she was
probably going to have to work with this one. Still, Ross
was going to find the pickings slim with my June.

He cocked his head interrogatively at Whitney and
said, "What can I do ya for?" Just the sort of locution one
might have expected, after the eyeing he'd given us. I judged
Barnett's age to be closer to my thirty-four than to Whitney's twenty-four, but he still contrived to project a charm-
ing-boy image, and it was not entirely unsuccessful. Even
with its obviously sexual overtones, I found it disarming.

I couldn't tell how Whitney was perceiving it. She
was a woman with a mission, and all her concentration
was on getting the information she needed. "Mr. Barnett,"
she said, plunging right to the point, "I'm doing research
on the Redland fire, and I understand you were involved
in it."

Barnett cocked his head again, letting a slight frown
slip across his features, though the smile stayed, too. "Involved?" he said.

"I heard you'd been one of the people most involved
with fighting it—"

"Ah!" Ross broke in, his face clearing. "Involved with
fighting it. Yeah. Yes, I sure was. Sure. What kind of research are you doing? I don't know that I could give you
anything that wasn't in the papers."

"I heard you were nearly killed."

Barnett nodded vigorously. "Yeah! Yeah, that's a fact, Miss Way. Way, didn't you say your name was? Sure, I know your family real well. I used to hunt over at Redland when I was working for the Forest Service down at Lufkin. Your cousin, I guess he must have been, Bob Jones? Yeah, he and I used to go out to a lease him and some other boys had, right out there behind where the old Redland Drive-In Theater was . . . ."

His deer-hunting reminiscences rambled on. From seeming fairly direct and businesslike, Ross Barnett's conversation had rapidly gone downhill into East Texas Old Home Week, and this hunting talk didn't seem to jibe with the gender-conscious approach he'd had when we first arrived. I wondered if East Texas women were easily seduced by what I would have classified as male-oriented talk. I'd have to ask Whitney about it. Local customs interest me. We are so much the products of our upbringing.

Whitney was doggedly turning the conversation back in the desired direction, and the information at last emerged that the Redland fire had taken place in the August of a summer whose climatic conditions had been very like those of the present one—"Dry as a Baptist deacon's likker cab'net," in Barnett's phrase—and after a show of puckering his forehead in thought, our entertaining informant finally came up with a date.

Since I thought that was all that Whitney had come for, I breathed a mental sigh of gratification at a goal attained and prepared to say good-bye, but to my surprise, Whitney seemed inclined to stay and talk.

Barnett invited us in with the offer of coffee, and she was going to take him up on it. I looked at my watch, and it told me I'd best hie me back to the motel if I was to be there at the hour appointed to meet June, and I truly did not want to antagonize her. I was secretly regretting having been so hard to deal with on this trip so far, and I wanted to let her know how much appreciated her patience with me really was.

"Whitney," I said, "I'm sorry, but I really have to get back."

"Aw, that's too bad, Miss Renfro," Barnett said with what sounded like genuine regret. "Heck, I haven't thought about those old days in a while now, and I was getting all wound up to talk. But if you gotta go, you gotta." He paused. "Hey! Why don't y'all drop in tomorrow over at the campus and I'll show you some pictures I've got of the fire damage and the boys that fought it and all? How about it?"

His engaging grin was hard to say no to and I was fascinated with his East Texas way of talking and would have enjoyed listening to more of it, but I really didn't know what my plans for tomorrow would be; they depended on June's entirely. I told him I couldn't promise, but Whitney accepted the invitation in a flash.

"Come on over to my office about eleven and I can show you what I've got there, and then maybe we can go eat lunch someplace more refined than the cafeteria. Like the Dairy Queen!" He laughed at his own joke, and so did we. I imagine that college cafeteria food is among the most universally maligned of cuisines the world over.

"And how old would you have been at the time of the fire," I asked Whitney as we drove back to the motel.

"I'd have been eight. I guess that's about the right size, the size I am in my dream."

"That old? You didn't have this dream earlier?"

"I don't guess so. Hell, T.D., I don't really remember. It just seems like I've had it all my life. But I just have no way of knowing. It could have started that late. Anyway, this fire thing is all the clue I've got about UFO's around here, so I'm going to follow that up."

"So what are your plans, then?" I asked. The slant of the sun through the pines along the streets of Nacogdoches threw long bars of shadow across the pavement. All was quiet, and there was a feeling of contentment about this town. I'd been slowly relaxing ever since we'd arrived. Now to communicate this feeling to June . . . .

"Well, the newspaper office, first thing in the morning, I guess, and then meet Barnett. And maybe by the time I see him, I'll have found out some stuff about the UFO business and can pump him about it.

She paused. "T.D., I don't know if I should really go on with this or not."

I looked at her, jarred from my reverie about June.

"I had another dream last night." She frowned, and I noticed her hands were very tight on the steering wheel. "It wasn't the same dream, the UFO one or whatever it is. This one was about . . . I guess it was about dangerous things in general. My mother was in it." (Whitney's mother had been dead for many years.) "I don't know where I was, somewhere I felt at home, anyway. But things kept happening, like something boiled over on the stove and I tried to push the foam back into the pot with my hands. Or I was going to, I wanted to, and then Mom told me, 'Whitney, you'll be sorry.' So I didn't do it, but I kept saying to myself, 'I've got to push it back, or it'll make a mess and ruin the stove.' And then I went outside and stood at the edge of a cliff and I was thinking, 'It's too far to jump.' And Mom called me, so I went back to the house, and everybody, all my relatives were there, and they were sitting down to supper like nothing had happened, and I knew I was the only one who knew about the pot boiling over."

She stopped talking and looked at me, waiting for a comment.

"Were you a little girl?" I asked.

"No. I was me as I am now."

"What do you make of this dream?"

"I don't know. I think it ties in with this stuff I'm trying to find out, though. Like a warning to myself not to mess around with it, because I might get hurt. And I think the part about the relatives sitting down for supper like nothing had happened was just me telling myself this wasn't a big deal to anybody but me."

"But it's a big deal to you."

"Yeah, it is." She concentrated on her driving. Then she said, reluctantly, "But that's not all."

"No?"

"No. I had another dream—or something."

I waited.

"It seemed like I woke up from that one dream, and there was somebody in my room."

"Who was it?"

"I don't know. It looked like a man . . . but . . . . It looked like a man with silver skin."

"Silver skin?" I kept my voice neutral.

"Yeah. Or a silver suit, maybe."

I waited for more, but she added nothing. She wanted me to get this out of her. "Could you see his face?" I asked.

"Well . . . I think so, but I couldn't really see any features. All I really remember is being afraid he was going to kidnap me. And I thought, over and over, 'You can't take me. You can't take me.' And then he was gone."

"He left?"

She knotted her brows, trying to remember. "No. He was just gone." She forced a smile. "So I guess it was a dream after all."

I smiled back at her.

"But it sure seemed real."

Then she firmly changed the subject. "God, T.D., it's good to be home!"

"Home in East Texas?" I said, pulling my attention back to the present.

"Uh-huh. Where the people talk right!" she said, exaggerating her East Texas accent, which no doubt had faded since her self-imposed exile to Austin. I smiled and so did she, and as I started to get out of the car in the red-dusted parking lot of the Pine Bough Motel, she reached over impulsively and touched my shoulder. "Thanks for going with me, T.D. It was nice."

"It was interesting," I said, and added, "I enjoyed it." And that was true. Getting out and seeing a little of the town and talking to at least one of the local people had been just what I'd needed to break me out of my sulk. I smiled warmly back at Whitney and we waved good-bye.

I walked with quickening steps toward the door of our room, and when I opened it and walked in, June was just in the process of changing out of her sweated-down clothes. I didn't waste words. I flung my purse and the room key on the bed and raced to capture her in my arms. We hugged hard, and I heard Whitney's voice in my head saying again, "It's good to be home!" I breathed in the familiar fragrance of June, snuggled my head against her shoulder, and said it aloud to her: "It's good to be home."

"Home?"

"Home. Oh, honey, right here." I nuzzled her neck and then looked up at her as she bent her face to me. "I love you, June," I said, and her arms tightened. Then she broke the embrace and pushed me back at arms' length, gripping my shoulders, unable to contain her excitement.

"T.D., it's just going to be great!" she said. "I can't wait to tell you about it. Gosh, it's just so exciting!"

"Well, tell all," I said, smiling back. June talking forestry school was like a schoolgirl talking about her first crush, and her infectious delight flooded the anxiety-darkened corners of my mind with healing radiance. Whitney Way and her nighttime visitations fled from my mind like ghosts at sunrise.

Chapter 9

I sat on the bed while June sat in a chair, and she talked. I half listened while I enjoyed the quick motions of her gestures and admired the squareness of her shoulders, the line of her thigh, and the graceful yet dynamic positions her body took as she shifted now and then, tucking one leg under her and hooking the other over the arm of the chair. I felt delighted in her nearness and her enthusiasm for life, and I wanted to kiss her, and stroke her . . . but it was easy to see that sex was far from her present concerns. So I took my thoughts firmly in hand and resolved to be patient and understanding. And just when I was consoling myself with the idea that maybe tomorrow we could take that walk in the woods I'd decided I wanted, she shattered my noble attempt at selflessness with the news, related in the same glad tone she'd have used to announce winning a national sweepstakes, that she was lucky enough to have been invited on an overnight field trip to see a forest of climax hardwoods, and that her plans were to leave in the morning and return the following day.

"*What?*" My exclamation of dismay startled her out of her narrative.

" 'What,' what?" she said, her puzzlement changing almost instantly to a kind of wary hostility. "Honey, I told you I might not be around much, once we got up here."

"Yes, but an overnight field trip? Honestly, June, doesn't that seem a little . . . cold of you? I mean, here I am, coming with you to see your new school and spend some time together, and now you tell me you're hurrying off to some forest of climaxes?"

"Climax hardwoods." Her voice was pointedly patient. "You see, as a forest evolves, the species which characterize it go from—"

"June."

"Well, hell. Damn it, T.D., you're obviously not a bit interested in this, so why do you encourage me to rattle on about it? If you think humoring me is going to make me decide to stay in Austin or something . . . ."

"Hell's bells! How could I make you stay in Austin? You're obviously set on this forestry thing, and obviously it's more important to you than I am, and—" She tried to break in, but I raised my voice and overrode her: "—there's nothing wrong with that! I'm not saying you ought to sacrifice your life to our relationship. All I'm saying is—"

I suddenly didn't know what I was saying. I really was, I realized, wanting June to live a less than fulfilling life with me in Austin rather than leave me and do what she really wanted to do. The realization of my truly unadmirable motives hit me like a blow to the mental solar plexus, if one can be said to possess such an organ. I stopped in mid-sentence and sat with my mouth hanging open.

June was glaring at me, waiting for me to go on and overwhelm her with guilt-tripping logic, but when the silence only lengthened, she finally said, "Well, go on. what are you *only* saying?"

I closed my mouth, at least, and gave my head a slight shake. "I'm sorry," I said, and I lay back across the bed and shut my eyes.

June said nothing. Then, after a minute or so, I heard her get up from her chair. I half expected to hear next the opening and closing of the door, but instead she came and lowered herself onto the bed beside me. I looked up at her and saw her gazing at me with speculation but without anger. I groaned and rolled myself into her arms, and we held each other without speaking for some time.

Later she patted me and asked if I was hungry. I said I supposed I was; I didn't really know.

"Well, I am," she said, getting up stiffly from the cramped position I had her in. She stretched out a hand to me, pulled me to a sitting position on the side of the bed, and leaned forward to brush a strand of hair out of my face. June, June! How heartbreakingly wonderful you are!

After we drove around Nacogdoches for a while, we discovered a cafe where the food was homey and generously served, even if the menu was a bit heavy on the greens, beans, and fried things. Afterwards we drove for a long time over the back roads through the piney woods. The peace and the blessed coolness of evening contented us, and neither of us mentioned the upcoming field trip. I was still too shocked by the discovery of the extent of my selfishness and my vulnerability to my lover to talk about it, and June, too, obviously thought the subject was best avoided. Instead, we talked about Whitney and Professor Barnett.

"Something struck me as peculiar," I told June. "He went right off into a long monologue on deer hunting, of all things, and that hardly seemed to fit in with his lady-killer image."

"Maybe he'd caught on that you were dykes, and he was treating you like some of the boys."

"I doubt it. Neither of us is all that obvious, except maybe to others of our persuasion."

June grinned at me. "You think not?"

"Why? You think I'm what the average heterosexual thinks of when he thinks, 'lesbian'? I hardly see that!"

"Oh, no." June took on her mock-serious tone. "It's just that when two unrelated, butch women turn up on the guy's doorstep—"

"Butch? You're calling me butch? What's that make you, King Kong?"

June laughed and scratched her head, monkey-fashion. I hit her.

"Why right now he's probably telling his buddies down at the barbecue joint, 'Boys, you shoulda seen them two gals. One of 'em just as cute as a bug, but that older one —now she might'a been short, but I'd hate to get that scrawny little red-headed thing in a fight!' "

"Capable and butch are not synonymous," I said haughtily, "and I'm hardly what one would call scrawny."

"You're not? I can feel your ribs," she said, reaching wiggling fingers toward my side.

I squirmed away and slapped her hand. "Watch your driving, nut!" I cried as she swerved almost off the road. "And as for my height—"

"Okay, okay, I know you're tall! Of course if you were any shorter, your feet wouldn't touch the ground . . . ."

"Damn it, see if I ever speak to you again!" I am considerably over five feet tall, by nearly three inches, at least. It was an old sore subject of mine which June had desensitized by kidding about it until now I could laugh with her.

"Seriously," she said when we'd gotten our breath, "Butch isn't bad, is it?"

"Hell, no, butch isn't bad! But, well, it's just that I'm not . . . well, not that much of a stereotype. You know what I mean?"

" 'We're not like them,' " she quoted. " 'We just happen to love each other and we just happen to both be women.' "

It was the traditional utterance of the homophobic lesbian trying to divorce herself from the rest of us who accept ourselves for what we are. June had a point. I really had been starting to sound like that.

This was about all the negative information I cared to learn about myself for one day. I was going to have to work through these unpleasant revelations sometime, but not right now. I changed the topic back to Ross Barnett.

"Well, whatever, something sure made him nervous for a minute there. He was talking fast, and I felt sure he was trying to cover some uncertainty or something he didn't want us to see. You may be right; it could have been that he was embarrassed about dealing with two dykes. Not *butches*, but dykes," I hastened to add. I ignored June's grin and went on. "I guess he could have picked up on us." I thought about that a second, then added, "But so often it's the relationship people pick up on, not something about the individuals. And Whitney and I aren't lovers . . . ."

June said, "Maybe not, but there's still a close relationship there, isn't there? The client-therapist thing?"

"But it's not what I would have expected a total stranger to perceive." I shrugged. "Oh, well. He got friendly again pretty fast, anyway. We're invited to lunch with him tomorrow, to look at his etchings."

"Etchings, huh?"

"Pictures of the Redland fire. Whitney's going to pump him about—it all," I said, checking myself just in time to keep from revealing my client's UFO fixation. I'd told June she was doing research on the fire, just as Whitney herself had explained to Barnett. Once in a while it gets hard to skirt around these things with somebody as close as June, but ethics and common sense demand it.

"Not the sort of thing I'd have thought you'd be very interested in," June observed, "but I'll admit Whitney seems attractive . . . ."

"Now, see here!"

June laughed at me for bristling, and I knew I'd have to avoid any reaction at all when she mentioned Whitney in the future. June loved to find a tender spot and keep poking it. Still, if she was teasing me, at least that meant she wasn't angry with me.

"Let's get back to the motel," I suggested.

"Are you getting tired?"

"No. Not at all."

June studied me appraisingly. "Not at all?"

"Not at all, darling."

She wheeled the car in a tire-squealing U-turn. "Time's a-wasting!" she said.

Chapter 10

How sweet love is when it's had a brush with danger
and come through! Our edginess with each other during
the day, our defensiveness and impatience and our un-
voiced but real fear that we might be losing something
precious, these things had threatened what we had between us and now, resolved at least for the moment, they
heaped fuel on the fires of our intimacy.

No sooner had we closed the door of our room behind
us than June swept me into her arms, her kiss fierce with
passion, and I met her heat with my own, pressing against
her and holding her hard, loving her with all my heart.
She gave a little moan, and the sound turned my knees
to jelly. We reeled toward the bed and half fell onto it,
June rolling me onto my back and tugging impatiently at
my clothes between kisses.

We hadn't made love for days in the rush and flurry
of getting the trip organized. June hadn't seemed interested, and I had been too distracted by the thought of her
leaving for school—and I was feeling too vulnerable to
risk that extra expression of closeness. But now her ardor
struck fire to my emotions as well as to my body, and the
rush of tenderness I felt for her blotted out all the worry
and the hurt, so that all I wanted was June, to be as close
to her as our bodies would allow, to fuse our beings in the
heat of our desires, separate but one, lovers and friends,
bodies and souls blazing together.

Breathing hard, I helped her get my shirt off, and my
bra, and she fell upon my breast with open mouth. Then

I was the one moaning, as she alternately pressed her face hard into the mound of my breast and then pulled back, eyes closed, holding my nipple between her lips and rolling its tip with her tongue now slowly, now in the quick, fluttery motion which I loved and which she knew I loved.

The feeling was wonderful — oh, more than wonderful! — but I wanted more and wanted it fast. I pulled June's hand away from where it was kneading my other breast and forced it toward the fastening of my pants.

"In a minute," she mumbled, holding my nipple in her teeth.

"Now!" Her hand resisted mine; I felt her strength, but the fire in me gave me strength of my own. I pushed her hand under the waistband of my pants, and letting go of my nipple at last, she raised her head and smiled.

"Impatient?"

"I want your fingers!"

"You do, do you?" Her hand wriggled under the tight cloth of my pants; the tips of the longest fingers played in the uppermost curls of my hair. Her eyes, hot and mischievous, never left mine.

"June, hurry up!"

She grinned. "Oh, I don't know. Let's wait a few minutes."

"June!" I grabbed her wrist and tried to force her hand down farther, but she was too strong for me, and the waistband of my pants wouldn't give any more.

"I'd like a snack before bed," she said, faking a move to get up. "Think I'll go get a candy bar. Do you want anything?"

"For God's sake, June," I yelled, wrestling her back to me, "just forget about any damn candy bar and undo my pants, will you?" I was lunging with my hips, trying to inch her hand closer to the target, but she was holding me down, though not without effort, and laughing at me.

"Wouldn't you like to watch T.V. for a while, and eat a nice candy bar? We can always get back to this later." But her fingers were inching farther into my hair, the tip of one just touching the beginning of the wet cleft . . . .

"A candy bar," I said through teeth clenched with the effort of the contest, "is not what I want to eat!"

I struggled frantically with the snap at my waist and got it open, jerked down the zipper, and was rewarded with June's fingers, freed at last from the restraints of the cloth, sliding quickly into my wetness and then in one motion plunging deep inside. She threw back her head with a groan, and I clasped her shoulders with both hands as I opened to her and took her in and came fast and hard to the pounding strength of her thrusting arm and the sound of her cries uniting with my own.

Then she held me, limp, still jerking now and then with little aftershocks of orgasm, with my face between her breasts while our breathing slowed and our strength returned, and we stroked each other and murmured endearments, flooded with tenderness for one another, and peace.

After a while June stirred and moved onto her back, and I followed and propped myself on one elbow, looking down at her, and then I undressed her slowly and carefully, gazing into her eyes all the while, and, the first wild urgency gone, made long, slow love to her with my lips and tongue and fingers until I had kissed and licked and breathed upon every part of her and followed my mouth with my hands, stroking lightly and then more urgently until she answered every touch with a shudder or a moan and her strong, smooth thighs squeezed my head convulsively for infinite seconds and at last fell limply open, still trembling now and then as my fingers brushed them.

We slept close that night, cuddled into the curves of each other's bodies. Had we known what the morrow held for me, we'd have packed up and left Nacogdoches as fast as my Mustang would have taken us. We had no way of knowing, of course. But it was to seem an eternity before we slept that way again.

Chapter 11

Early morning in East Texas. The clean, cool scent
of pine, lightly overlaid with the dry odor of red dust.
The light a transparent gray, casting no shadows. Complete stillness, except for a far-off birdsong and the occasional swish of a passing car.

Wrapped in my bathrobe, I stood at the door of our
room and watched June loading her suitcase, camera, note-
books, and binoculars into the trunk of my Mustang. Excitement had awakened her early. She broke into a smile
when she turned and saw me there.

"I was going to wake you," she said.

"Are you all packed and loaded?"

"Um-hm. Do you feel like driving me over to campus
to put these things on the bus?"

"Let me dress." I'm not at my best when I first wake
up. June was accustomed to it and didn't try to converse.

In the bathroom I passed the back of my hand across
my face, enjoying her faint, lingering scent on my fingers.
If I could have taken her back to bed right then I would
have, but instead I sighed and reached for the hand soap.
Best to be a realist.

We kissed before we went out to the car. It wouldn't
do to be too open here, we agreed. And all too soon we
were drawn up at the curb behind the bus and I was shutting the lid of the trunk and facing June, awkwardly laden
with her belongings, and saying a formal good-bye.

I always find such moments difficult. What I want
to do is to give her a hug and a kiss and tell her I love her

or even just say something like, "Have a good time, honey!"
And if I were a man, or if she were, I would. If I were a
man. Or if the world were the way it ought to be. If we
weren't afraid, always, to be seen to care.

"Have fun," I said, telling her the rest of it with my
eyes.

"Thanks. You, too."

We stood and faced each other for a scant few seconds.

"I'll be back after lunch tomorrow."

"I'll be glad to see you."

"Well. 'Bye!" She grinned and winked and turned
toward the bus, and I climbed into the Mustang and drove
away. It had already been as long a good-bye as I cared
to subject myself to.

And now here I was at some ungodly hour of the morning, in a strange town where I didn't know a soul and had
nothing whatever to do, with a whole day and a whole
night (which didn't bear thinking about) and more than
half of another day to kill. Presumably the university had
a library, so I supposed I could at least go there and read.
And I'd have to find meals for myself, which might be
interesting, and Whitney had told me something about
some local sites important in Texas history; in despera-
tion I might visit those.

And then I remembered. Whitney, of course.

Professor Barnett's invitation to lunch and etchings
had presumably included me, and it seemed as good a
plan as any. I had no idea how to get in touch with Whitney, but she had said she was going to the newspaper
office, so maybe I could catch up with her there. I wouldn't
even mind reading some of the old files to help her in her
search. I needed the distraction of some company.

Actually, I found her in the coffee shop where I decided to have breakfast. She assumed I'd noticed her car
in the parking lot, but I hadn't, being mostly oblivious to
things mechanical.

"I've already done a little from the newspaper angle,
last night," she told me when I spoke of plans for the day.

"They were very nice about letting me come in right before five and just stay while they put the paper to bed. Look what I found."

She handed me a folder which contained copies of several news articles, some with pictures of the people involved. There had certainly been a UFO flap going on in the area around the dates of the Redland fire, and quite a flap it had been. Dozens of residents for several miles around Nacogdoches and Redland had reported seeing lights in the sky, mostly at night or in the early evening hours, but there were even one or two in broad daylight. These were written off by "authorities"—the sheriff's and police departments—as airplanes or stars or, in one improbable case of a bright light which had seemed to be flashing in Morse code (as reported by the observers, who admittedly didn't know Morse code themselves), as a prank by college students.

"Have you found anything about the rumor that the fire was started by one of these things?" I asked Whitney, handing the folder back.

"Not yet. I still have some looking to do. I haven't worked up to the actual dates of the fire, yet. I was starting at the first of the summer."

"The earliest of these you found was July?" I said, thinking back over the dates on the stories I'd seen.

"Yeah. The middle of July. So that would put it about a month before the fire."

"And today you plan to work forward from there."

"Right. I still don't know how I'll tell if any of these things pertain to me. I guess I'll just keep reading and maybe later chart the sightings out on a map or something. I'm just feeling around in the dark." She knitted her brows. "I still feel nervous about this. I can't forget those dreams."

"Did you have any more of them last night?"

She shook her head. "Slept like a baby." She cocked an eye at me. "I guess you and June are doing something, so I won't ask you to give me a hand."

"Truth to tell, I've been abandoned." I filled her in on June's field trip. "So, if you'd like some help, I'm free," I finished.

My offer was accepted with alacrity.

The newspaper office was one of the more bustling places I'd seen in Nacogdoches, but, true to local form, the people seemed actually happy to see us and interested in helping with our search. Whitney being already familiar with the procedure for looking up material in the morgue, we got down to business right away. Except for the occasional newspaper employee who wandered by to glance at what we were doing and inquire whether we had everything we needed, we were alone there, seated at opposite ends of a library table so that each of us would have room to spread out our papers.

"Isn't this a cheerful place, for a morgue?" Whitney said as she showed me how to go about things. "I guess a newspaper's pretty human. They put it to bed every night, and when its one day of life is over, they take it to the morgue."

"Why not call it the mausoleum, I wonder?"

"Because it isn't really buried yet, and people like us can still dissect the news and learn something from it?"

"The forensic pathologists of news," I said.

We settled into companionable silence. While Whitney journeyed methodically onward, date by date, from where she'd left off last night, I adopted a more intuitive approach. Taking papers she'd already looked through, I tried to get a feeling for the atmosphere of the time and location and an idea of the people here. I wasn't really interested in UFOs so much as in learning about what to me was an unfamiliar culture, and newspapers were a good way to do that. Once a lover and I had planned to move to Maine (until her potential job there had fallen through, to my secret relief), and we'd subscribed to the York County Coast Star, a local weekly, through which we came to feel quite at home in that place we'd never actually seen.

Now I amused myself with local controversies and economics, ads and obituaries and births and lists of who had been admitted to the county hospital. Whitney was uncovering more UFO stories, and finally she got to the Redland fire itself.

There was extensive coverage, of course. It had been the biggest forest fire in these parts for decades. She copied the articles on the newspaper's copier and then handed the papers to me to look over before stacking them to be re-filed.

"I can't find anything yet about how the fire started," she said, handing me a paper. There's something there about our Ross Barnett, though."

Indeed there was. Ross Barnett seemed to be the spokesman for the Forest Service. He was quoted again and again, on the subject of the fire's rate of spread, the action along the fire lines, on the plans for containment. There was even a picture of him, looking very young, with black smudges on his face and his hair in disarray. There were other articles on the equipment and techniques being used in fighting the fire, including DC3s flying over the fire and dumping water on it, the use of bulldozers to clear firebreaks, and the special heat-resistant clothing furnished a few of the firefighters at the most dangerous parts of the fire line. Volunteers had come from all over East Texas and western Louisiana to try to contain the Redland fire. This was the kind of thing I liked reading, people helping each other in the face of danger.

There was also a brief mention of a fire-connected death, a Forest Service employee who had been cut off by the fire when it first started. I went back to the paper from two days earlier and read the original story. Here, too, Ross Barnett was speaking for the Forest Service, but his involvement was more personal.

The dead man, Jeff Andrews, had been with Barnett when they discovered the fire. Andrews had skirted the fire in one direction while Barnett had taken another logging road to find out the fire's extent. The story quoted Barnett in an interview:

" 'The wind shifted and caught him,' Barnett said. Barnett himself was able to escape in a jeep over disused logging roads, incurring only singed hair and some smoke inhalation. He was treated and released at the hospital emergency room. Recovery of the body of Andrews will not be possible until the fire has either been contained or has burned out in that immediate vicinity."

So Ross Barnett had had a near escape. I wondered how well he knew the man who was lost, if they'd been friends or hunting buddies or just co-workers. The fire had started, we knew, on the deer hunting lease owned by Barnett's friend, Whitney's cousin.

"Have you asked your cousin about how the fire started?" I asked Whitney now.

"Huh?" She broke away from what she was reading, raising her head slowly toward me while her eyes hurriedly finished scanning a line or two, then finally looking up.

"Didn't our professor say the fire started on your cousin's hunting lease?"

"Oh." She marked her place with a finger. "Yeah. Cousin Bob."

"Have you asked him about it? It seems as if he ought to know all this, oughtn't he?"

"I suppose. But I haven't seen him. He wasn't at the family reunion. I think they said he had to work or something. He does maintenance at the sawmill."

"Oh." We went back to our reading.

Then, "Ha!" said Whitney. "Here it is!" And she shoved an article under my nose. "Flying Saucers Fire Cause?" awkwardly queried the headline. Three Redland residents, according to the story, claimed to have seen a bright light swaying over the woods close to where the fire had been discovered the following day. They were certain the "flying saucer" had started the fire, ". . . because it couldn't have been campers, since that's private land, and it couldn't have been a cigarette, because there's no road in there, and there wasn't (any) lightning (at the time the fire was thought to have started.)" Ross Barnett, described as a spokesman for the Forest Service, had commented that the cause of the fire was unknown and would be investigated. He refused to speculate further than to make the observation that private land was not immune to trespass.

Barnett hadn't seized on the UFO as the explanation for the fire, and his comment about trespassers led one to believe that he thought the fire had a human origin. But even though we glanced through as many more days of the local paper as we had time for, neither of us found an official statement on the cause of the Redland fire.

"Let's go ask him," Whitney said, stretching and looking at her watch. "I could use some lunch, too."

Saying our farewells and expressing our gratitude to the office staff at the paper, we sallied forth to see Professor Barnett's etchings.

Chapter 12

And pretty impressive "etchings" they turned out to
be. The few blurred pictures in the Nacogdoches paper
had given not the slightest idea of the destruction of the
fire compared to the Forest Service photographs Barnett
spread out before us. Especially horrifying were some pictures of a logging operation underway in the location just
a few months before the fire and comparison shots taken
of the smoking ruin of the forest afterwards. It had been
an area of mature pines with very little undergrowth to
mar the cathedral-like impression of the huge, straight
trunks that dwarfed the loggers and their equipment. After the fire, a few black trunks still jutted upward from
the ghastly rubble, tapering to points where the branches
had burned away. In one shot the body of a deer lay in
the foreground, so charred as to be unrecognizable were
it not for the magnificent and fire-blackened rack of ant-
lers lying askew, partially burned from the skull.

I shuddered.

"Not pretty," said Barnett quietly.

"No."

"It was no fun taking these shots, and then when I
developed them and printed them, it was like living through
it all over again." He closed his eyes, then opened them
and grinned. "I'm used to them, now," he said.

"How could something that can run like a deer get
caught by a fire?" Whitney frowned at the photograph.

"Sometimes the wind shifts or gusts suddenly. Nothing can really outrun a forest fire like that one. Trees way

out in front of the fire itself get so hot they explode. Pines have a lot of resin. It's flammable.''

"You had a close call yourself, didn't you?'' I asked.

Barnett half-smiled and nodded his head. "As a matter of fact, I did.''

"The paper didn't say much about it,'' Whitney put in.

"The paper?'' Barnett looked surprised.

"We've been looking over the articles about the fire at the newspaper office,'' Whitney explained.

"Boy!'' Barnett grinned. "Y'all really mean business, don't you? Say, what are you doing with all this, anyway? Working on a paper for some class?''

"Uh . . .'' Whitney said.

"Whitney's a history buff,'' I said, giving him a reassuring smile.

"And local history seemed like something I ought to know about, especially since I was a little girl when the fire happened,'' said Whitney, taking up the same tack. "I feel like I ought to know about things that happened in my own lifetime that affected my hometown and my family, don't you think?''

Barnett looked slightly amused. "I guess so. History's not something I've ever thought too much about, myself. Though there's been some pretty interesting things that have gone on in this neck of the woods. Like the New London School Disaster, and things like that.''

"Yeah, that's a famous one. I guess everybody knows about that. A gas explosion, wasn't it?''

And they talked for a gruesome few minutes about the horror that had overtaken that country school so long ago. Barnett seemed to feel genuine sorrow as he recounted stories he'd heard about the explosion, the deaths, and the grief. I upped my estimation of him a notch. There was real sensitivity under the good ol' boy facade, and he had was not afraid to let it show.

Getting back to the subject of the forest fire, Barnett slipped the photographs back into their envelope and said, "It looked pretty god-awful then, but today you'd never know it, if you hadn't seen it before the burn. Looks just like the rest of the woods around. The trees are young, of course, but pines grow fast.

"I'd like to see it," Whitney said.

"Well, I believe your cousin Bob still has it leased. I don't know why he wouldn't let you in there. It's interesting to see how different it's come back from what it was. For instance, you saw in the logging pictures how clean the understory was? How little brush was in there? Well, now there's a whole lot more little hardwoods of different kinds—a lot more piney woods than pine woods. That all gets started when the big trees are burned or cut off. Otherwise, they shade out all that little stuff."

"I wondered why they were called the piney woods instead of the pine woods," I said.

"Well, now you know," said Barnett. "Hey! Y'all want to go get some lunch? I'm hungry enough to eat a mule and chase the rider!"

We laughed with him and left the office.

At the restaurant—a quiet, ordinary cafe not in the least like the Dairy Queen—Whitney said, "Professor Barnett, how exactly did the Redland fire start?"

"How'd it start?"

"I didn't see anything in the paper about it, at least not any official statement."

"No. I don't think any official statement was ever issued." He busied himself with his salad.

"I thought the Forest Service was going to investigate . . . ."

"Well, yeah, we did investigate, all right. But we never could come up with anything conclusive, officially. It was a hot burn, not much left where it started."

"But you have some idea?" Whitney wasn't going to let him off the hook so easily.

"Well, it could have been anything."

"Like what?"

Barnett looked a bit uncomfortable. "Oh, it could have been a lightning strike. We'd had a little thunder the night before. Or it could have been somebody walking in the woods there. People don't realize it, but just throwing away a cigarette or even a match can set the woods on fire, especially as dry as it was. Just about like it is now. We're all sitting here chewing on our fingernails and praying for rain before something like that happens again. We've been real lucky so far.'' He sipped his iced tea and grinned at Whitney. "You're really getting into this thing, aren't you? Are you sure this is just historical curiosity?''

Whitney smiled. "Well, maybe I have a little more personal interest than that.'' Her glance caught mine, then shifted back to Barnett. "Actually—'' She took a sip from her glass of tea, swallowed, and blotted her lips with her napkin, then went on, "—actually, I was wondering if you thought there was anything to . . . well—'' She laughed, glancing again at me. "It's a little hard to say it—you're going to laugh at me.''

"Try me.'' Barnett smiled encouragingly.

Whitney gathered her courage and plunged. "Well, I know this sounds stupid, but I noticed there were a lot of things in the papers about people, ah, seeing things in the sky. Lights, or, ah, something. And somebody said—''

Barnett laughed. "Oh, yeah, I know what they said. A couple of pulpwood cutters told everybody that'd listen that they saw a flying saucer over there and naturally that's what must have set the woods on fire. Boy, we had a time getting *that* fire put out! We had about fifty or sixty calls after that particular word got around, people wanting to know if it was true, or if it was a government secret experiment and if the government was going to pay everybody damages—hell, I could have strangled those old boys with my bare hands, if they hadn't been twice as big as me and four times as mean! Anyhow, if you're thinking it was a fire bug from outer space, all I can say is, it's the first one of those I've ever heard of, and forest fires have been my bread and butter for twenty years.''

"Well, I knew it sounded silly,'' Whitney said, embarrassed, "but I thought I'd ask, anyway. And you know, there were a lot of reports of UFOs in the paper about that time.''

"Well, we don't have much news around here."

"Oh."

I decided to come to Whitney's aid. "So you don't believe in UFOs?" I asked.

"All I know is, I've been outdoors most of my life and I've never seen one. Oh, I've seen a lot of weather balloons from the launch site over at Palestine. But nothing I couldn't identify. No little green men or anything." He chuckled. "I expect most of those flying saucers come out of a bottle."

Whitney was sawing at her chicken fried steak with her knife and giving that task all her attention. My heart went out to her. She had the UFO idea so firmly in mind that I suspected this kind of talk seemed almost like a personal attack. So even though Barnett was saying virtually the same things I'd always thought myself, I nevertheless felt compelled to challenge him, not so much in the interests of science as to put my client at ease.

Drawing on my recollection of the information I'd gleaned from the TV interview I'd watched and the discussion between Caroline, Roya, and June (Roya! Her attractive face flashed automatically across my mind, but was instantly replaced by the memory of June looking down at me in bed last night), I waded in where those conscious of their reputations for rationality normally fear to tread.

"Surely," I began, "we can't write off all the UFO sightings as weather balloons—"

"Hell, no!" Barnett broke in laughing. "Some of 'em are just a bunch of publicity-seeking crazies out to get their picture in the paper."

"But the UFO contactees I've seen on television certainly impressed me as intelligent, rational—"

"Oh, sure. Crazies come across that way. I've known some crazies in my time, believe me. When you deal with people every day like I do, you meet all kinds. Believe me, not everybody's over at Rusk that ought to be there!"

Rusk was the site of a state mental hospital. I saw Whitney wince.

"I deal with people myself," I said, understating the case, "and I really don't believe that all those who say they've seen these things are crazy, or publicity seekers. It seems to me that one would really have to believe he'd seen a UFO to go public with it, considering that yours is probably the prevailing attitude in society. The ridicule must be quite punishing."

"Yes, exactly. You'd have to be crazy to let yourself in for that!" Barnett said triumphantly.

"T.D., if we're going to talk to Cousin Bob, we'd better get going," Whitney said, making a show of looking at her watch.

"You're right," I said, although this was the first time I'd heard we were going to see Cousin Bob. "Mr. Barnett, thank you again for your help. It's been very interesting." Whitney was already pushing her chair back and getting up from the table.

"Y'all are going out to see Bob Jones?" Barnett asked.

"We're going to look at the sight of the fire," Whitney said, her voice artificially bright.

"Well, have a good time," Barnett said. "Watch out for flying saucers out there. You don't want to get carried off to Mars or something!"

He laughed, I smiled politely, and Whitney gave a sarcastic smirk, which I believed Barnett took as approval of his humor. He picked up the check, we thanked him for lunch, and we all walked to the door together.

"It's been nice meeting you both," Barnett said. "Holler if I can do anything else for you."

I laid a hand on Whitney's shoulder, steered her out the door, and gave her a sardonic smile from the side of my face away from Barnett as I waved him good-bye.

"We don't have to go see Cousin Bob if you don't want to," Whitney said as we walked toward our cars. "I just had to think of a reason to get out of there."

"I don't blame you! He was laying it on pretty thick."

"Yeah. And it wasn't just those two guys that saw that thing over the woods that burned. A lot of people saw it. My own cousin saw it." She sighed. "Well, anyway,

I'm going to go out there, for whatever good that might do."

"Actually," I said, surprising myself, "I would like to go with you. I do want to see the woods as long as I'm up here. They're all June talks about." And if June was having a field trip, I was going to have one, too.

"Great!" said Whitney. "It'll be great to get back in the woods again." She flashed me a smile that stopped just short of having a wink with it. "—Especially with my therapist to protect me from the little green men!"

Chapter 13

We went back to the motel to change into woodsier clothes. Whitney brought her bag in from the trunk of her car and laid it on the bed. I selected jeans from my suitcase and one of June's T-shirts, as being more appropriate for roughing it than any top I'd brought, and stepped into the bathroom with them.

When I came out, dressed for the wilderness, Whitney was sitting on the edge of the bed and pulling on rough-out western work boots. She had on jeans and a short-sleeved white shirt, which she had yet to button. It hung open enticingly, revealing a white cotton bra contrasting with smooth, lightly-tanned skin. I looked away, thinking of last night. The memory of making love with June was still very specific and quite physical in its effect.

"I love your car!" Whitney was saying.

"Thank you." I watched her get up, stamping her feet to settle the bottoms of her pants over her boot tops. She started to button her shirt.

"I've always loved the way old Mustangs look, but I've never ridden in one."

She was buttoning her shirt from the bottom up. I noted her slim-fingered, dexterous hands. Hands are a sort of a thing with me, lesbians' hands especially.

"Why don't we take my car, then?" I said, taking her hint.

"Super!" She finished buttoning and wriggled her shoulders to straighten the fit of the shirt, tugging at the tails so that the material tightened across her breasts. I drew a long breath. No harm in looking, I reassured myself. I smiled, thinking of what June would say. But June would never know. Not that I was ashamed of my thoughts; they were perfectly natural and I wasn't going to deny them to myself. But June would have entirely too much fun with them. In any case, it wasn't as if I were actually fantasizing any sort of physical relationship here, and even if I had been, I know the difference between fantasy and reality, and —

T.D., you old dog, you, I said to myself. I smiled at Whitney and held out the keys. "You'd better drive," I said, "since you know where we're going."

Her face lit up like sunshine.

And drive she did. Her delight in my car delighted me afresh; it was a very satisfying car to drive. Through the dark lenses of my sun glasses I watched the glare of the midday sun dancing off the long, vibrating hood in front of us and relaxed happily. The day I'd thought would be boring was turning out to be interesting and fun. I had good company, and I was enjoying seeing some aspects of Whitney which didn't often surface in the clinical atmosphere of the office: her playfulness, her acute interest in her surroundings — and of course, the artless way she buttoned her shirt, I reminded myself wryly.

"I don't think Professor Ross Barnett quite knows what to make of us, T.D.," said the subject of these thoughts, breaking into my reverie.

"I agree, but what makes you say that?" I was always interested in comparing my observations of a situation with those of others.

"The way he talked when we went over to his house, for one thing. All that stuff about deer hunting. It just didn't seem to fit in with his male chauvinist girl baiting. Or was it dyke baiting? Do you think he spotted us?"

"I wondered the same thing at the time," I said.

"But we aren't that obvious! At least, you're sure not. I guess he could have spotted me, if he'd been looking for it. But you don't look like most people's idea of a dyke, with the way you dress and do your hair . . . ."

"Don't tell me I don't look like a lesbian, now Whitney!"

She blushed slightly. In our professional relationship we of course talked personally about her, but that had never worked the other way. The focus in the office was on Whitney. Now I was turning the tables on her, watching to see how she handled it.

She handled it very well, after the first blush. "T.D., I won't lie to you," she said, a twinkle in her eye. "You do look like a lesbian, but a certain *type* of lesbian."

"And what type might that be?"

"The competent yet feminine type."

"As opposed to the incompetent yet unfeminine type?"

She laughed. "No, as opposed to the fluffy yet feline type!"

I nodded solemnly. "Or the shaggy and canine type."

"But definitely not the horsy type!" She laughed again and so did I, as we both glanced at my admittedly small-boned and non-athletic frame.

"No," I agreed, "definitely not the horsy type. I am not of the sporting blood in any way, shape, or form."

"Far from the madding stereotype." She flipped on her turn signal and slowed as we approached a red dirt road which intersected the paved one we were on. "But you drive a classic car," she said. "That's pretty sporting."

"For its looks alone, I'm afraid. I've been thinking about getting an MR2, if this one gives me any more trouble."

"No kidding? You'd trade in your Mustang on a Toyota? Oh, T.D.!" It was obvious that I had gravely disappointed her.

"It's been refusing to start a couple of times lately," I explained, and, as the car suddenly juddered with a great racket across some corrugations in the hard dirt surface, "This is not the best road in the world!" I continued.

"Sorry. But believe me, it's better to take it faster than

slower. This way we go across the tops of the ridges, but if we slow down, we'll hit the bottoms of the valleys, too."

A cloud of red dust boiled up behind us, and the pines close along the shoulders of the road already showed a heavy, brick-colored coating from cars which had passed before, further evidence of the summer drought.

"Your cousin certainly lives out in the country," I said, holding onto the arm rest to steady myself against the jolting ride.

"It's not far now," Whitney assured me. "Just over this hill and across the creek."

The creek in question was not wide and was spanned by a rumbling wooden bridge of boards laid crosswise, with two sets of planks on top of them paralleling each other along its length to accommodate the wheels of the car. Things were rapidly getting more primitive than I had been prepared for. I began to wonder if Cousin Bob's home would be a log cabin with an outhouse behind it.

It was no such thing. A neat house of brownish brick, set back among the pines, with two late-model pickup trucks parked in the unexpectedly paved driveway appeared on our right, and Whitney braked smoothly and brought us to a stop, turning off the engine and handing me the keys as our trailing dust cloud caught up with us and lazily enveloped the car as it settled.

"Thanks for the ride," I said.

"My pleasure, ma'am," said Whitney, bowing and, I thought I detected, blushing a little. This was a small role reversal for us. Even in client-centered therapy, the client accords the therapist a certain amount of power — puts her in the driver's seat, in a manner of speaking. But in this instance, it was still my car, a fact of which of course we were both aware, and that made the dynamics of the situation quite different from yesterday's, when Whitney had driven me in her own vehicle . . . . Maybe this was actually a fairly close analogy to letting the client control the content of the session while the therapist controlled the location, the duration . . . . I'd have to think more on this interesting metaphor when I had time.

We got out and I followed her up the path of concrete stepping stones to the front door, the heat already moistening my skin with perspiration in the short walk from the air-conditioned car. The screen door was unlatched, and Whitney opened it and walked in, calling, "Hello-o! Anybody home?"

Voices, male, were coming from a room deeper in the house, and we went toward them. Before we could make out any words, we could hear the relaxed, easy cadence of conversation punctuated by low-key laughter. The room where the men were talking was a den, set down a step from the rest of the house, with glass doors opening onto a patio in the back. A large brick fireplace, filled at this season with an arrangement of artificial flowers in colors brighter than I would have chosen, formed the centerpiece of the room. On the mantel a white wooden cutout of a goose dressed in checked gingham sat cheek by jowl with a pair of ceramic kittens, an entirely un-Dresden shepherdess, and a bronze German shepherd dog on a marble base. The brick over the mantel bore a black cast iron American eagle with a banner in its beak. Besides this fireplace, the other focal point of the room was a large console television set wearing an elaborate crocheted doily starched into voluminous ruffles, in the center of which nestled a pressed glass bowl of plastic fruit.

On one wall an electric clock designed to look like a huge pocket watch was closely hemmed in by a collection of framed family photographs including wedding pictures, silver-haired couples, two boys in high school football uniforms, a girl in an academic gown and mortarboard, and three babies, two in studio poses and one naked on a rug. The other major wall space was taken up almost entirely by a large print of a romantic landscape scene featuring mountains, water, and trees, and complete with dripping elk or some such animal submerged to its knees in the mirror-like lake.

The occupants of this remarkable setting were two men in jeans and T-shirts reclining in La-Z-Boy chairs, smoking, and drinking Budweiser. One of these gentlemen was about my age, dark haired and sporting a mustache, while the other was older, greying, with a clean-shaven but craggy face which looked as if it had been left outdoors in all weather. It was the younger of these who spoke first.

"Cousin Whitney! Well, come on in here, girl!" His smile of welcome looked open and genuine, and he tipped his chair upright and held out a big hand.

Whitney shook it, introduced me by name but not by title or profession, and greeted the other man, who turned out to be her uncle, Jimmy Cowley, the non-talkative one whose manner, she had told me, had frightened her as a child. He smiled pleasantly enough, if not with the same enthusiasm as his younger relative, and in a bass voice said he was pleased to meet me. I saw him look from me to Whitney with what seemed to be a glint of speculation in his eye. Whitney might be in the closet to her relatives, but that closet might well have a glass door, I thought.

Whitney came right to the point of our visit. "Bob, T.D. and I wondered if you'd mind if we walked around on your deer lease a little bit."

"My deer lease? Sure, that's fine . . . . Y'all just looking to get out in the woods?" He cocked his head in much the same way as Whitney often did. A family mannerism, I assumed.

"I wanted to show T.D. what it's like. She's never been here before."

"I'm an old West Texas girl," I put in. "I grew up around Lubbock, and we don't get too many stray pine trees out that way." The easy rhythms of Texas small talk emerged in my speech with surprising facility. "This is just a lot of lumber on the hoof, to me," I added.

"Oh, yeah," Bob said, nodding vigorously, "the South Plains. I been up there a time or two myself. You sure can see far! Matter of fact, I was driving up to Lubbock one time at night, dark night, just as black as the inside of a well, and I come up over that caprock and, boy, there was lights just as far as the human eye could see. All little towns, I guess, and then I drove until I liked to give up before I ever got to one of 'em. You wouldn't think you could see town lights that far!''

"Grow cotton up there, don't they?'' said Uncle Jimmy, entering suddenly into the conversation. His gruff voice and unexpected speech startled me. I could see how a child might find him threatening.

"Yes. Quite a lot of cotton,'' I agreed.

Uncle Jimmy jerked his head in an abbreviated nod and chewed on his unlit cigar.

"Used to be cotton country around here, though you might not believe it,'' said Bob. "But the War Between the States didn't do the business no good.'' He chuckled. "Anyhow, that land up there where you're from's already cleared!''

"How exactly do we get to your lease?'' Whitney interjected. "We don't have very long.''

"Y'all in a hurry? Heck, I remember when we were kids, you used to spend all day out in those woods if your mama would let you,'' Bob said.

"Did I?'' Whitney said, looking puzzled. She hadn't told me anything about spending time in the woods.

"You don't remember that? Why Whitney, we used to call you the Indian, you spent so much time out there by yourself. Don't you remember, when we'd all be over at Aunt Louise and Uncle Jimmy's and you'd get off in those woods to some secret place you had and your mama'd about have a fit trying to find you? Boy, girl! You used to get in trouble with a capital T about that! And you say you don't remember it?''

Whitney shook her head.

"Well, I'll swan! I r'member one time, must of been when you were about eight or nine, 'cause I know I was in high school, anyway, and we'd all been over there for Aunt Louise's birthday or something like that, and anyway, you went off, and when your folks got ready to go home, your mama 'bout had a cat over you being out in them woods with your Sunday school clothes on. Whewee! I wonder you don't remember it! I know you come in

73

with some pine rosin or something all on your dress, and I told you if brains was gasoline, you wouldn't have enough to drive a piss ant on a motor scooter halfway across a dime, and you got so mad at me I thought you was gonna beat me up, little as you was."

"Well, *I* don't remember that!" Whitney said, her smile showing through a mock frown. A familiar camaraderie between her and her cousin was clearly evident.

"Could'a grown cotton on that deer lease, right after we had the fire over there," Uncle Jimmy growled abruptly.

Immediately, if I read him correctly, he regretted this entry into the conversation, because he pulled a lighter out of his pocket and retreated behind a blue cloud of pungent cigar smoke, and I had to make a mental leap backward to realize that this comment was not a non-sequitur to Bob's reminiscence about Whitney's solitary forest jaunts but instead the continuation of the thread of small talk about growing cotton on the South Plains because the land was already cleared. The fire had certainly cleared the land where it burned, but Uncle Jimmy, I recalled Whitney's saying, was the one reluctant to talk about the fire. From his referring to it now I could see that it must be on his mind, at any rate.

"Uncle Jimmy," Whitney asked, jumping at this opening, "didn't anybody really ever figure out how that fire started?"

"Lightning," said Uncle Jimmy with finality. He picked up his beer and drained the can. "Well, I got to get out of here. Nice to meet you," he said, nodding at me. "Whitney, come and see your Aunt Louise before you get away." He unfolded from the chair and stood up startlingly tall, well over six feet, towering over me by more than a foot. I hadn't realized how tall he was when he was sitting down, probably because he was so brawny in contrast to Cousin Bob, who was much more lightly built.

I smiled up at him as winningly as I could, getting good eye contact, and told him it was nice to meet him, too. I got a quick elevation of the corners of his mouth and a little crinkling of the skin around his eyes in reply. My impression was that Uncle Jimmy was more inclined to like people than he wanted to let on and was capable of going to great lengths to hide this vulnerability. My client Whitney had often displayed the same tendency. I thought if I could get Uncle Jimmy talking, he might well come through with some information Whitney wanted, but there seemed no chance to waylay him at the moment.

"What's the best way to get out there?" Whitney was saying as I watched her uncle depart.

"Heck fire, Whitney, don't tell me you don't remember that!" Bob exclaimed. "Why, it's those same woods you used to play in, girl!"

"Well, it's been a long time, so refresh my memory," Whitney said impatiently.

"You just go out past Jimmy and Louise's and turn in at the first gap gate on the left. It's got a lock on it, but the combination's 6-3-3-9. Just be sure to keep it locked, okay? You can drive on in there on the fire roads and pretty much get around the whole place in your car, if you want to."

Whitney thanked him, and we said our farewells and made our exit.

With Whitney once again behind the wheel, we retraced our route to the paved road, turned onto it, and followed it for a mile or so before we again swung into a dirt lane flanked by dusty pines. On the way I asked Whitney about the tale her cousin had told about her playing Indian in the woods alone. Could her dream memory have something to do with that?

"The hell if I know. Bob and I were pretty close as kids, even though he was quite a bit older than me. But I really don't remember going out and playing by myself in the woods. I guess I did if he says I did. Maybe whatever scared me so bad made me forget all about it."

"It must have been really scary, if it made you forget something you used to like to do so much."

"If it was anything like my dream, I know it was."

We approached a white frame house on property cleared of all trees except an obviously planted one of some kind growing in the front yard. "Aunt Louise and Uncle Jimmy's," Whitney said, nodding toward it. "Listen, T.D., would you mind if we stopped for just a minute so I can say hello to Aunt Louise? I haven't seen her this trip, and I'd hate for her to think I didn't care enough to stop in."

"It's your excursion," I said. I wasn't too crazy about getting out into the actual woods, anyway, although the idea that we could see it all by car mollified me somewhat. I recalled June's talking about needing insect repellent on her field trip to ward off ticks and chiggers, and the thought of delaying an encounter with these unpleasant creatures made a visit with Aunt Louise vastly appealing. "I'd like to meet your aunt," I added.

"We won't stay long," Whitney assured me.

"I'm in no hurry," I hastened to say. "Take all the time you like!"

Chapter 14

This house was older than Cousin Bob's, and I found it somehow more pleasant, though it, like his, was not air-conditioned. Yet even with the stifling heat outside, the temperature in the dining room into which Aunt Louise ushered us was quite bearable, made so by the breeze coming through the tall windows and, I thought looking up, the fact that the ceilings were quite high, somewhere in the neighborhood of twelve feet, so that the hottest air rose well above our heads. What it would be like in the winter, I shuddered to think, but it was a practical design for the East Texas summer climate.

The dining table where Whitney and I pulled out chairs and settled ourselves was large and round, suitable for big family meals, and covered with a plain white cloth which showed a carefully darned place here and there. Aunt Louise, having greeted Whitney with evident pleasure and a hug and me with a cordial smile, vanished through a swinging door into what I presumed was the kitchen, talking all the while.

"I was just making a grocery list. Johnny and Lou Ann and the kids are coming for dinner Sunday after church — Whitney, hon, would you and your friend like cream and sugar? I've got some angel food cake—" The swinging door muted the sound of her voice for a moment, then allowed it full volume as it swung back, admitting our hostess bearing a tray laden with a coffee pot, cups and saucers, and a plate with about a third of a tall cake. "—This is a bakery cake; I meant to bake something for my prayer group yesterday, but I got busy putting up some figs and didn't have time, so I just ran in to Lufkin and picked this up—"

Whitney and I made effusive noises of approval and anticipation.

"It's so good to see you, Whitney! I wished the other day at your grandma's house I'd have had time to talk to you more, but you know how those reunions are, you don't get to talk to near everybody you'd like to, and you have to listen to some you'd rather not!" She winked at me. "Are you and Whitney staying up here for long?" she said.

I opened my mouth to reply as Whitney said hastily, "T.D. is up here with a friend of hers from Austin, and we just happened to run into each other. They're staying in Nacogdoches."

"My friend is going to study forestry at Stephen F. Austin in the fall," I added.

"Oh, how exciting! There're several women working for the Forest Service now. And are you going to be in school, too?"

"No. No, I'm still working in Austin." I wasn't going to get into the subject of my profession, lest it make Whitney uncomfortable, but Aunt Louise persisted.

"Oh?" she questioned, interested. "And what kind of work do you do?"

"I'm a psychotherapist."

"Oh, my! That must be so interesting! But isn't it upsetting, working with mentally ill people? I'd think it would be just so distressing . . . ."

"I don't really work with the kind of client most people would think of as mentally ill," I explained.

"Therapy can be good for anybody," Whitney said. "You don't have to be crazy. Lots of perfectly normal people are in therapy."

Aunt Louise said, "Well, I can think of a few around here that could use an all expense-paid trip for one to Rusk!"

"We're going out and walk around on the deer lease,"

Whitney said, changing the subject. "T.D.'s never had a chance to get out in the woods and see what they're like."

Aunt Louise smiled at me and said, "Well, T.D., Whitney's the one to show you around, all right. She used to have all kinds of hidy-holes and secret places out there when she was little."

"So I hear," I said.

"Oh, yes, she was a little wild Indian!"

I thought I'd broach the flying saucer subject and see if the aunt could tell us what the uncle wouldn't, so I said, "Mrs. Cowley, Whitney was telling me about some rumors of UFOs in this area when she was a girl. Do you remember anything about that?"

Whitney raised her eyebrows at me in surprise, but sat a little forward to hear what her aunt would say.

"UFOs? Oh, the flying saucer scare. Why that would have been fifteen or twenty years ago. Yes, I surely do remember. I saw one myself!"

"You did?" said Whitney.

"Mm-hm," Aunt Louise confirmed, nodding proudly. "I surely did. It was right out back, here, right over the barn, a great big light shining right down on the roof of the barn. It was in the evening, right after supper, just when it was starting to get dark, and Johnny—that's my boy, he and Lou Ann, that's his wife, and their kids, they're the ones that are coming to Sunday dinner, I was telling you," she broke in for my edification—"Johnny was in the house, and I hollered for him to come and see it, too, but he never heard me, I guess. Anyway, he didn't come.

"I just couldn't take my eyes off that thing. I never saw anything like it in my life. I must have watched it, oh, I don't know how long. It didn't seem very long, but the next thing I knew, it had gone off somewhere and it was already dark, so I must have watched it longer than I thought. But that was right before I got all that eye trouble, my eyes just swelled right up and kept watering for about a week, and Jimmy—that's my husband—he never would believe me. He said it was just my eyes playing tricks on me. But I saw that thing, all right. I heard it was some

kind of an army thing or other, some kind of a defense
secret that they were testing up here. Of course, Jimmy
thinks it was just a weather balloon.''

"That's what he said the other day,'' Whitney agreed.
"We saw him over at Bob's just now.''

"He goes over there to drink a beer, I know." She turned
to me, dropping her voice conspiratorially. "I won't have
it in the house, here. But Jimmy thinks it's all right to
drink it, and I can't stop him. So he does it over at Bob's.''

"About when was it you saw this light or whatever
it was?'' Whitney asked.

"Let me think." Aunt Louise pursed her lips and drew
her eyebrows together. "Well, it was not too long before
the forest fire. We had a big fire here,'' she explained to
me, "and it burned all around this place. It was a wonder
the house didn't go. But you know most of our land is
cleared, anyway. This used to be part of a big farm, Crys-
tal Farm, it was called. It's pretty much farmed out land,
but anyway, that's why it doesn't have many trees on it.
It was lucky for us it didn't, because that's all that saved
us from burning up. Johnny and I wet down the roof, and
the roof of the barn, and we beat it back when it tried to
get started in the field over yonder." She gestured toward
the window. "Jimmy was fighting it with the Forest Service, of course, but they didn't have enough men to spare
us any here. Y'all better eat up the rest of this cake; it's
just going to get stale.''

I declined while Whitney took another piece, and Aunt
Louise poured more coffee in our cups and went on.

"You remember that, don't you, Whitney? In fact,
seems like you and Connie and maybe Bob were over here
when that fire first started. It's a wonder you weren't out
there; you were always in the woods if you could slip
off.''

"I wasn't out there, though, was I?''

"No. I don't guess you were. Your mama came to get
you and take you home, and it seems like we had to look
for you but we found you in the barn or someplace. I don't
really remember. That was before the fire started coming

this way. I remember they said the wind changed, and
that's what brought it over here.''

"I don't remember that,'' Whitney said.

"Well, you were just a little girl,'' said her aunt. "I
guess you had other things on your mind.''

It was another twenty minutes before we could make
a graceful exit from the hospitality of Aunt Louise and,
affirming our intentions to come again the next time we
were in the area, get into the car and make for the deer
lease.

Since Whitney was driving, I saw it was my duty to
get out and open the gate when we pulled into the sandy
ruts leading into the property. I hadn't known just what
Cousin Bob had meant by the term, "gap gate,'' but I was
about to be educated. The fence was of barbed wire, and
the gate was merely a continuation of the fence, but instead of being set into the ground, the posts in the gate
section were loose and the end one was connected to a
gate post at one side by a pair of barbed wire loops, one
at the top and one at the bottom. The technique, obviously, was to slip the top loop over the top of the post and
then remove the post from the bottom loop and pull the
freed fence section to one side so that the car could drive
through.

This process is difficult to describe accurately, but
even so it was easier said than done. Whoever had constructed the gate had intended it to be used by someone
bigger and stronger than I. The lock Cousin Bob had told
us about fastened a chain around the movable end of the
gate, but once that was undone, I was at an impasse with
the barrier. I pushed, pulled, grunted, and came hazardously
close to pinching my hand between the wire and the post
but made no other discernible progress, and finally Whitney got out of the car and helped me. Between the two of
us, we got the contraption open. She drove the car through
and then got out again and we tackled the infernal thing
to close it. It was a good thing Whitney was taller and
heavier than I. Our combined weight, pushing with all
our might, was barely enough.

We got back into the car streaming perspiration. This so far was not the comfortable automobile tour of the forest I had been anticipating. I directed the air-conditioning vent at my face and sat back limply.

"That was the hard part," Whitney said.

"I should hope so!"

She grinned at me and put the car in gear.

The woods were lovely, I had to admit. It might or might not have been cooler in the deep shade of the pines; I didn't plan to roll down the window to find out. But the the brown carpet of pine needles on the forest floor was dappled with sunlight, the mid-level spaces were crowded with undergrowth whose bright green leaves, flecked with light, seemed frozen in dance against the somber background, and above these the trunks of the pines rose to dark green crowns which admitted shafts of filtered light to the levels below.

"It's beautiful," I said, and Whitney nodded, driving in silence.

The road led us into the depths of the forest, and after a few minutes Whitney stopped the car. "Would you like to get out?" she said.

I thought of ticks and chiggers and snakes and wild beasts, and then I looked at Whitney's face and saw her eyes soft and her brows relaxed, her perpetual tension gone, and I said, "Yes, let's do."

And I was glad we did. With the engine switched off, the silence of the place was hard for my city ears to believe. We couldn't hear anything but an occasional whisper of breeze in the pines high above us, a far-off bird song, and once in a while the light tick of a pine needle cluster falling to the ground. We walked into the trees away from the road on ground which descended in a gradual slope, and after a minute or so Whitney raised her hand and stopped, looking carefully about her. "I thought that's where we were," she said.

"Where are we?" I asked quietly.

For answer, she moved on, motioning me to follow, and I did so.

Ahead the trees thinned and the light increased, and to my surprise, when we had forced a narrow way through a tangle of brush and vines, we emerged on the low, sandy bank of a gliding brown stream.

"The Angelina River," Whitney said. "I remember this place now. Boy, the river's low."

Not knowing the usual depth to expect, I had only to look at the banks and the muddy sandbars to see that the stream had often been higher than this, though there was still a channel which looked deep enough to me, accustomed as I was to the shallow, rock-bedded rivers of the hill country.

"You remember this from when you were a little girl?" I asked, still keeping my voice quiet.

"Yeah." Whitney's tone, too, was hushed, wondering. "I'd forgotten all about this until just now, when we started down that slope. No wonder they didn't want me out here by myself. I could have drowned, or got bitten by a water moccasin, or —"

"Water moccasin?" I said in a controlled tone.

"Yeah, there's a lot of them in there. See, this place backs right up to Aunt Louise and Uncle Jimmy's. Now I remember we could only go as far as the old fence —there used to be an old fence through here, someplace over there, but I guess it's long gone now, with the fire and all — but I used to sneak off and come down to the river. And if I remember right—" She strode away along the edge of the mud with me following hastily, scanning frantically for poisonous reptiles. "— Yeah! The road comes down and turns along the river, and there was a fishing dock where Uncle Jimmy kept his boat . . . there!" We rounded a clump of brush and faced a wooden dock built high above the current level of the water but reaching out far enough to get to the main channel. An olive drab boat, flat bottomed and square of ends was tied to one of the posts that supported the dock.

"Would that still be your uncle's boat?" I asked.

"I bet so." She turned to me grinning. "Wow, T.D., I remember this!"

"And do you remember anything about the dream, now?"

She looked thoughtful. "I don't know. There was something, but I can't get hold of it." Then her face cleared as the smile came back, and she said, "But who cares? This is great, isn't it? Wow, T.D., it's like coming home!"

"Isn't that just what it is?" I asked.

She smiled at me, and the look in her eyes was dreamy and peaceful. "Yes," she said. "That's just what it is. And I know things are going to be all right."

I returned her smile. It's wonderful to see a client feeling good. "I know they are, too," I said, and added, "provided we don't meet any water moccasins!"

Our laughter rang cheerfully through the woods.

Chapter 15

"Come on up here." Whitney clambered onto the wooden dock and turning, stretched her hand to help me up. "I used to sit here and watch turtles and stuff in the river," she said, walking to the end of the boards and lowering herself to sit with feet dangling above the water. Hesitating while I took in first the rough surface of the dock, which I decided looked clean enough and free enough of splinters not to do much harm to my jeans and anatomy, and then the water below, which seemed free at the moment of predatory creatures, I sat down beside her.

"It is good to be home, T.D." She swung her legs idly, gazing out over the flowing stream. I watched it, too, fascinated by the slight swirls and wrinkles in the surface which were the only indication of the current. The water was noiseless in its passage, though now and then a faint splash came to my ears from somewhere. Some water creature, I assumed, rising for air or a look around, or slithering off the mud bank.

"Turtle," said Whitney, pointing. I looked and then saw a small something holding its place against the current: the turtle's head. As we watched, it vanished suddenly and silently, making hardly a ripple.

How long we sat like that I don't know. It could have been ten minutes or it could have been twenty. I thought of watching June's pet koi in their pool at home. Tame, they would come to the side of the pool to beg for food, and June would kneel at the brink and feed them by hand, talking to them and calling them by name. What would I do with the fish when June was gone? Feed them, of course. And think of June every time I did. Or would she want to find them another home, with someone who would appreciate them as she did? I supposed I could put goldfish in the pool to keep down the mosquito larvae, once the koi were gone. Goldfish wouldn't take much attention. Oh, June!

We needed to talk, June and I. I felt a surge of impatience with the field trip that was taking this time we could have had together, time we needed. I also felt impatient to the point of acute irritation with June for going. She was going to have the rest of her life to traipse around in the woods looking at trees. This was a time we should have been together, talking about our relationship and our future — or futures, plural, separate futures . . . .

I had been unconsciously picking at a splinter on the edge of the board I was sitting on, and now I ripped it off and flung it viciously into the stream. Here I was sitting in the wilderness, not with my lover, but with Whitney Way. Instead of a vacation, I was spending all my time with a client, and I couldn't even look at my watch and end the session. I didn't even know my way out of these damn woods without her.

Whitney, no doubt noting the violence of my splinter-flinging gesture, looked at me curiously. I smiled, rather tightly, I'm afraid, and pretended not to know that she had noticed. The splinter floated slowly away, turning lazily on the current.

" 'Dark brown is the river,' " Whitney quoted, " 'Golden is the sand . . . .' "

I knew the poem, but I hadn't thought of it for years. My mother used to read it to me when I was a little girl, and I took up the relevant lines. " 'Boats of mine a-boating,' " I said, and together Whitney and I queried, " 'When will all come home?' "

We were pleased with ourselves for our literary recall.

"I think that was green leaves that were a-floating, not wood splinters," Whitney said.

"Irrelevant detail," I replied.

"I'm home now," she said. "I never thought I'd come home like this. God, T.D., I've missed this country! And I've missed the people. My Aunt, and Uncle Jimmy with his cigars, and Bob always kidding me, and my sister and my mom — and even people like Professor Barnett, who's just a good ol' boy. But I *like* good ol' boys! I know it's not politically correct, but I just get along with people like that."

"You seem quite at ease," I said.

"I am. Really it's almost enough to make me think of coming back here to live, except that I know what would happen if these nice people found out I'm a dyke."

"What would happen?"

"Well . . ." She studied the water for a minute or so, thinking. "With some of them it would be okay. Not okay, really, but they wouldn't really reject me for it. They'd just figure it was a tragedy for me, and they'd be careful not to mention it in my hearing. And some just wouldn't care, because they'd figure they didn't have much to do with me, anyway. But there'd be some that'd care a lot. Some of those good ol' boys I enjoy so much. Some of them could be downright dangerous, not just unpleasant about it." She sighed. "So I guess I'm stuck in Austin, because I don't think I could detach myself that much from what people think."

"That isn't easy to do."

"No. And I don't want to, anyway. I care about people, and I want them to care about me."

"Even people you disagree with?"

"Even them. Some of them, anyway." She flashed a sudden grin and added, "Even people who think UFOs that shine lights down on barns and cause time losses and conjunctivitis are weather balloons! T.D., could you believe that? Aunt Louise really had a classic lost-time contactee experience! It all fits. She called Johnny and he didn't come. Well, that's classic. They sort of 'switch off' anybody they don't want witnessing what goes on. And the eye trouble. That happens over and over, in everything you read. The light causes conjunctivitis like that. It's right out of the books, T.D."

It certainly went along with the little I knew about these phenomena. I was beginning to think there was something to Whitney's UFO dreams or memories that couldn't be written off as a masking device covering some ordinary childhood trauma. I wished I had enough training in hypnosis to follow it up through that medium. Or did I really wish that? I wasn't sure that UFOs were really what I wanted to deal with. Whatever they were, they were definitely unpleasant to encounter, and Whitney's had even included an implied threat of death. Weather balloons, I reflected, didn't do that.

"Okay," I said, squaring off mentally to do battle with the flying saucer problem, "What do we have so far?"

"About the UFO, you mean? Well, let's see. We have my dreams. And that vision or visitation or whatever it was the other night, about the silver-suited guy in my room. And we have the documented UFO flap around here at about the right time of my life. We have the forest fire connection—that the UFO was suspected as the cause of the fire, and that Aunt Louise saw the thing right before the fire. And I was at her and Uncle Jimmy's place the day the fire started, too. And I used to play out here in the woods that were burned."

"And the cause of the fire was never determined," I added.

"Right. So it really could have been the UFO, and I could have been right there. It all fits, doesn't it."

"It seems to. But there are other ways of looking at it, Whitney."

"What other ways?" She frowned at me.

"Think about this. All we know is that there was a forest fire and that there were UFO reports about the same time. Both of those things would probably have impressed a young child, and both of them could have been very frightening, especially since the fire involved places that were very special to you."

"You mean I could have drawn some connection in my own mind about the UFOs and the fire and come to believe that the UFOs were really after me?"

I nodded. "I wonder how you felt about disobeying your parents by sneaking off into the woods alone?"

"Hmm." She was silent for a few moments, thinking it over.

"Suppose," I went on, "that you were really out in the woods when the fire started."

"I'd have been scared to death. But . . . ."

Her voice trailed off. I waited to see where her thoughts would lead her next. It seemed obvious to me that a plausible (and intellectually preferable) alternative to UFO-induced memory loss was repression of the memory of the fire arising from Whitney's fear at having been in danger of getting caught by it herself, coupled with guilt at having disobeyed her parents about being out alone in the forest. When she spoke again, however, she put forth a suggestion for which I was not prepared.

"Oh, god, T.D." She looked slightly sick.

"What is it?" I said gently.

She turned stricken eyes on me and spoke with growing horror in her voice. "T.D.," she said softly, "what if *I* started that fire?"

Chapter 16

"Daisy Renfro, give me those matches!" My mother's voice, angry, threatening. The box of Fire Chief matches trembling in my hand behind my back. I looked up, tears already brimming over my eyes and running unchecked down to my chin, beginning to drip onto the front of my cotton print playsuit. My arm moving slowly, almost against my will, bringing the awful, forbidden box into sight and holding it up to that implacably outstretched hand. The memory ended there, before the inevitable spanking, a cameo of shame — Daisy Renfro, aged probably about four, disgracefully discovered in willful violation of a cardinal rule: Don't ever play with matches.

I sighed, and turned to Whitney Way. "Do you think you did start the fire?" I asked. With the calm in my voice I sought to soothe her fear.

She shook her head. "Couldn't I have? Couldn't that be why I've forgotten it all so completely? I do that, you know — forget unpleasant things. You know I do that, T.D."

"I know you do. But that doesn't seem like enough evidence to accuse yourself on." I laid a hand on her shoulder. "Let's think about this, Whitney." I said. "How do you feel when you think about fire?"

She thought a moment. "I don't guess I feel much of anything. I mean, I guess it would depend on the circumstances. I light the stove all the time. I can't say I feel anxious about it or anything."

"And how about wood fires? Do you ever light a fireplace fire, or a campfire?"

"Yeah, once in a while. I used to go camping a lot when I was with my first lover." She grinned. "But what I worried most about was whether I was going to be able to do it with one match, without using newspaper. It was a point of honor to use just wood kindling and one match. I got that from Girl Scouts."

"So the idea of fire in itself doesn't bother you."

"I guess not." She paused. "But in a way, it does, too. Because every time I'm away from home, I always think the house is going to burn down while I'm gone. Well, not every time, but when I'm out of town, for instance. I always kind of hold my breath when I come back until I can see that it's still standing."

I pondered this.

"Hell, T.D.! You know how I always feel like everything is going to fall apart if I'm not right there holding it together, anyway. Maybe this fire thing is just an expression of that—and I know I need to work on that," she said, heading off any such suggestion I might have been tempted to make.

I smiled at her. "We can leave that until later," I said.

"Fine."

"But right now, do you remember ever having a camp fire when you were playing in the woods as a girl?"

She shook her head. "No. I doubt that I did. I was forbidden to play with matches, and I know my parents made a point of talking about the danger of forest fires. I even had a Smokey the Bear teddy bear." She shrugged and turned her hands palms up in a dismissive gesture. "Who knows?"

"Maybe this is something that will come back to you, now that you've been here and started to remember."

"Maybe. But God, what if I really did that?" she said, her anxiety returning at once. "Those pictures Professor Barnett had . . . those beautiful trees . . .. It's enough to make me afraid to go to sleep tonight. I don't want to dream about . . . that."

I didn't blame her. I remembered vividly, myself, the pictured devastation, and particularly the carcass of the deer. With an inward shiver, I remembered something else as well. It had not only been a deer that died here. There had also been a human casualty. Fortunately Barnett hadn't shown us a photograph of his co-worker, or what must have been left of him after they found his body. Even the briefly imagined image, which I thrust out of my consciousness as swiftly as it arose, had seared itself with stomach-turning detail into my brain.

"If you have any bad dreams," I told Whitney, "you can call me at the motel." I only hoped I wouldn't have any nightmares of my own. There was no one for me to call.

We walked back to the car by the road. Whitney drove, and we followed the soft sand ruts as they wound through the woods and at last rejoined the way we had come in. The gate was no easier this time, but we tackled it together and at last we were through it and locking it behind us.

Neither of us said much on the way back to Nacogdoches, since we were both tired and hot, and we each had things to think about. Whitney said she was going home to her mother's house, looking forward to some East Texas home cooking. I thought I'd find a new restaurant or maybe just pick up a hamburger and a paperback and hole up in the motel room, escaping into a good read. At least it would be indoors, and I had every reason to expect it to be both vermin- and varmint-free. I felt sticky and grimy and unfit for human companionship, unless that companion could have been June, and of that there was no possibility.

After Whitney, having delivered me to the Pine Bough Motel, had returned my keys with renewed praise for my Mustang, started her own newer and less-stylish car, and driven away, I let myself into the room, flipped the window air conditioner to Max Cool, and flopped across the bed. A shower was what I needed, but first I felt I would just rest for a minute. I wouldn't even close my eyes . . . .

It was the last slanting bars of light from the setting sun striking my eyelids through a chink in the curtains which woke me. I dragged myself up and into the shower, and then, dressed in less survival-type gear than my woodswoman togs of the day, made my way to the Dairy Queen and then to a convenience store with a paperback rack.

The selection was dismal. Harlequin Romances are not my style. Neither are international espionage novels, or the ubiquitous drug-dealer, vice cop episodes which the popular taste currently feeds on. I did at last find a Freeman Wills Croft reprint which I seized thankfully, but on closer inspection I discovered I had read it. Despairing of finding anything suitable, I gave the revolving rack a final whirl and found myself face to face with a silver-suited being decorating the cover of a book which promised to recount in harrowing detail the experiences of a number of UFO contactees. Nothing more promising being offered, I picked this up, carried it to the counter where I paid the presiding college student, who took my money with a friendly word and only a semi-lascivious smile, and bore my purchase home to my lonely room.

There I installed myself in the arm chair to devour my DQ Dude and french fries—I discovered I was absolutely ravenous after my trek in the outback—and opened the UFO tome to its introductory chapter.

Sigh. As I had all along thought, the world of UFOlogy was not for me. Something was obviously at work in these cases, but extra-terrestrials couldn't account for the bizarre stories the contactees told, or if they did, these e.t.'s must be either diabolically evil or the morons of the universe— or think we were.

But where did that leave my client, whose veracity I had no reason to doubt? She wasn't making up her dreams. Her mind was hiding something from her, whether UFO encounter or frightening experience of a more ordinary kind. I would help her discover that secret if I could, when she was ready. At any rate, she was certainly motivated, which made her rewarding to work with, and of course I quite liked her, as well.

Still, lacking any entertainment but the UFO book, unless one counted Saturday night television, for whose blandness I was not in the mood, I read desultorily along from chapter to chapter. Then in one account this sentence struck my eye: "The object at once took off vertically, *leaving no evidence but a circle of burning brush.*" Oh, boy. Or "I'll swan," as Whitney's cousin Bob would have said. (It had taken me a while to realize that this was a euphemism for "I'll swear," as "heck" is for "hell," "darn" for "damn," and so on. "I'll swan" was really getting serious about the Biblical injunction against swearing, refusing not just to do it but even to admit one *would* do it.) Anyway, I had been ready to "swan" that no UFO had ever been known to start a fire, and here was a case right before my eyes. "Whitney, my girl," I said aloud, "perhaps you weren't playing with matches after all."

I sat there staring, unseeing, at the page of the book, eyes unfocused. In the ever-vivid theater of my mind I watched a huge ship hovering over the forest, a silver-suited being approaching a frightened little girl, the light from the object blinding and paralyzing her and the knowledge being injected into her brain, perhaps by some form of telepathy, that to reveal what she'd seen would mean her death. The dead body Whitney had reported "remembering" was probably a projected symbol chosen to convey to the small human the concept of her own mortality. In my mind I saw with her young eyes, and I felt her terror, as the silence of the forest was broken by the great, sudden roar of the ship accelerating away—

"AHH!" I yelped, leaping in my chair. The bedside phone shrilled again, and I scrambled across the bed and snatched it before it could have a third shot at my screaming nerves.

"Hello, darlin'." June's voice was husky, intimate.

"You scared me out of six years' growth!"

"Huh? What do you mean?"

I told her, briefly, what I meant: "I spent the day out in the woods, where several years ago there were a lot of UFO sightings, and then I was reading this book about

that very same scary subject, and I was definitely not ready
for the phone, which has a ring calculated to wake the
dead, to suddenly screech in my ear. Anyway, how are
you?"

"Great! Wonderful! Oh, honey, this is just so . . . so
exciting!"

I felt myself smiling, heartwarmed at my lover's delight. Then what I'd said sank in, and June said, "Wait!
Did you say you spent the day out in the woods?"

"Correct, my dear. I thought if you could do it, so
could I." I thought swiftly about what I could say without
betraying client confidentiality and went on to tell her
that Whitney was interested in the UFO flap that occurred
when she was a little girl and its possible connection with
the Redland forest fire.

June didn't think much of the UFO angle, but she was
interested, as I unfolded my tale, in my impressions of
Professor Barnett, and she particularly enjoyed Whitney's
assessment of him as a "good ol' boy."

"He's supposed to be a top-notch teacher and an authority on forest management," she said. "Everybody likes him
or hates him, from what I hear. He used to work for the
Forest Service, before he came to Stephen F."

"He worked for them at the time of the Redland fire,
in fact," I confirmed. "I think I told you. He almost got
killed by it, I understand. One of his co-workers did, actually. Why do some people hate him?"

"Male chauvinist stuff, I gather."

"Good ol' boy! But he's not insensitive, I think. And
he did buy us a good lunch, while being fairly obnoxious
about the UFO angle."

June laughed. "Well, honey, I doubt you'll find a forest management specialist who wants to consider the danger of fires from flying saucers!"

"Are you laughing at me, June?"

"Mm-hmm."

"I thought so."

"Do I gather you're dealing with this extra-terrestrial
stuff in the context of Whitney's therapy?"

"Whitney finds it interesting," I said. "So do you, for that matter. So did Caroline and Roya."

"So she has contactee syndrome, huh?" said June, smugly ignoring my attempt to evade the question. "That's a new one for you, isn't it?"

"I never heard of 'contactee syndrome,' and you know very well I'm not going to talk about what I'm doing with my clients, so just pipe down, smarty pants!"

"I can give you a reading list on UFOs if you like; I know you'll want to be well-informed. I understand some people in your field make a specialty of contactee work."

"June . . . !" I said warningly.

She burst into giggles. I did, too.

"Actually, I did hear some scuttlebutt about Professor Barnett," she said, controlling herself, "from one of the older grad students. He's been a Forest Service employee for donkey's years, and he said Barnett wasn't too well thought of in some circles there."

"Oh, no? Why would that be?"

"I didn't milk him for all the details, but he mentioned something about Barnett's being very ambitious and getting passed over for some kind of promotion or something. That's why he left the Forest Service, apparently. But ambition never hurt anybody in academia, did it? He's probably right where he wants to be, now."

"He seems content," I agreed. "But I have no real way of knowing. He did show us some gruesome pictures of the Redland forest fire. June, you won't end up fighting forest fires, will you?"

She heard my concern and hastened to reassure me. "It's not as dangerous as it sounds, sweetheart. It's not like going into burning buildings when the roof might fall in on you or something."

"Yeah? Well what about these trees that explode with burning resin way out in front of the fire? And what about the way the wind can shift suddenly and roast you to death and they have to wait for the fire to die down before they can even get your body out? And then it's all black and horrible, and —"

June whistled softly. "Wow, honey, who've you been listening to?"

"Professor Barnett, who should know, having been nearly killed that very way himself, and his friend actually was! June, oh, I wish — !" I broke off before I said too much. She knew how I felt, and it wasn't going to change her mind.

Her voice came to my ear, soft with tenderness. "T.D., honey, I'll be fine. Just fine. And I love you very much, T.D."

"I love you, too, June."

And that's what this whole conversation had really been about. We loved each other and we were going to be separated, and we were both afraid.

I went to bed soon after we'd hung up. The motel sheets were smooth and cool and the bed was wide, and I lay in the middle of it so it wouldn't feel so empty. I stared at the ceiling in the faint green light from the neon sign outside, breathed deeply, and relaxed limb by limb, clearing mind and body of the tensions which kept me from rest. Then, lacking a Smokey the Bear teddy bear to comfort me, I hugged my pillow, snuggled my face against it, thinking of June, and went to sleep.

Chapter 17

I slept blessedly late in the morning, and awakening, stretched and smiled, realizing I'd slept well and that today June would be back in my arms. Empty, indeed, my arms felt, though I lay for a few minutes hugging my pillow and thinking explicitly of what I'd be doing if the pillow were June . . . and of what she'd be doing to me. Rested and content together, we would cuddle and snuggle, sleepily talking. And perhaps talk would lead to caresses, and those to kisses, and kisses to intimate stroking, and that, perhaps, to staying in bed all morning.

But on the other hand, maybe we'd just get up and get dressed and go find someplace to eat breakfast, which is what I, in June's absence, proceeded to do. I was famished. I thought maybe pancakes, with ham and eggs and homemade biscuits, all washed down with plenty of fresh, hot coffee, might do well to pass some of the time until June's group got back.

The cafe I found to provide this repast was downtown, and I parked my Mustang on the red brick street and followed the aroma of coffee through a door whose brass handle was polished by generations of hands and which opened into a delicious-smelling place where a mixture of college students and locals, the latter mostly of a much older generation than mine, clinked their china and silverware amid a friendly babel of talk. I took a booth along the wall, ordered coffee, and studied the menu. It offered everything I had in mind, and having given my rather comprehensive order when the waitress returned with my coffee, I sat back to absorb the local color.

The service was friendly, the food was good, and I enjoyed a pleasant and leisurely repast. By the time I had finished and paid my check, the morning had worn on to the point that I was beginning to see passing outside cars whose occupants were, from their formal raiment, homeward bound from church, and I was more than ready for June's bus to return. I decided to go to the campus, walk around a bit, and wait for it.

As it turned out I should have retired to my room with my UFO book instead, but who knows how things might have developed then? The motel might have been destroyed by a tornado out of the blue, or the first earthquake in the recorded history of East Texas might have brought the building down around my ears. That might possibly have been worse than what did happen. Possibly. At any rate, I exited the friendly cafe, slipped behind the chrome-spoked wheel of my Mustang, and drove to the serenely forested campus of Stephen F. Austin State University.

I parked behind the forestry building where the bus would arrive, then strolled around on the broad sidewalks, enjoying the pleasant atmosphere. Since it was Sunday there were few people about. I found the Old Stone Fort, which Whitney had told me was a local point of interest. It didn't seem like much of a fort, but I did admire the little red sandstone building, liking the way it seemed to fit so perfectly into its East Texas environment. In Austin the limestone buildings give the same impression of rightness, almost growing out of the rock of the hills. This building—I couldn't think of it as a fort, though I assumed it must at one time have had some kind of fortifications around it, like the Alamo—was a stronghold in the Fredonian Rebellion, which was the first stab at Texas' independence from Mexico. No trace of glorious struggle lingered now.

It was while I was walking away from there and looking idly for something else to occupy me until time for June to return that fate took a hand.

"T.D.!" I turned to see Whitney getting out of her car. "Good morning!"

I watched her as she hurried to meet me, looking boyishly feminine—"gamine" may be the word I want, but I have never liked it; it has always seemed to me to have a sort of biological ring, like "gamete"—in her jeans and T-shirt, apparently braless today, her breasts as well as her silky, brown hair bouncing with her steps. I reflected that the sight of her would turn heads of either sex.

"Wow, we keep running into each other!" she said, catching up with me and slowing to a walk.

"So we do. And where are you bound, this Sunday morning?"

"I thought I'd see if the library was open. They might have some stuff on UFOs I haven't found in Austin, I thought. Anyway, I thought it would be worth a look. Where are you going?"

I told her, and we strolled in companionable silence for a few paces.

"Did you have a nice evening?" she asked.

I said I had, my mind scrolling back through the reading, June's phone call, and the wide, empty bed. I mentioned only the Dairy Queen hamburger and going to bed with a book.

Then she said, a little reluctantly, as though she'd been holding it back, "Well, I got drunk last night."

I raised an inquisitive eyebrow.

"After supper I went over to Bob's. You know, he and I used to be pretty close as kids."

"I know you were."

"But it's funny, we hadn't talked for a real long time, years, I guess. Anyway, he had beer, of course, and we got to drinking and smoking—cigarettes only!" she interrupted herself, seeing the surprise on my face.

"I didn't know you smoked cigarettes. Is this a new habit you've acquired?"

"Oh, not really. I smoke at parties and stuff. Anyway," she hurried on, putting an end to that line of discussion, "we had a great time. Talked about all kinds of things. I found out more about different cousins and aunts and uncles than I ever knew. And poor Bob found out more about the Austin lesbian community than he ever wanted to know!"

"You were in a confidence-sharing mood."

"You could call it that! I lost count of how many beers I drank. Really I don't usually just get drunk, T.D. But last night I guess I was so wound up—you know all that stuff about finding out things I'd forgotten and getting out in the woods again and then thinking that . . . that about the fire . . . ."

Her voice darkened at the end of this recital. I wasn't at all sure in my mind that her idea about having something to do with starting the fire didn't have some truth in it; at least it would neatly account for much of her fear and the repression of all memories about her play times in the woods. Still, there were other elements, particularly in her dream, that didn't fit that hypothesis. We'd need to talk this out, but back in Austin in my office, I hoped. I certainly didn't want to get into the middle of it and then have to break it off when June's bus came in. Also, I could practically hear June laughing at me about all this free therapy I was passing out and kidding me about playing in the woods with my attractive young client. June was sometimes prone to tease a bit near the bone.

"Anyway," Whitney went on, picking up her tempo again, "we can talk about all that stuff next week."

I breathed a mental sigh of relief.

"But I did pick up some interesting gossip about our friend Professor Ross Barnett."

"And that was . . .?"

"Well. It seems he used to work for the Forest Service at the same time my uncle did—you knew that—but there was a big deal about him wanting the job my uncle got. See, Uncle Jimmy got the job that Jeff Andrews was supposed to get."

"Jeff Andrews?" The name sounded familiar, but who was —? "Oh. The man who was killed?"

"In the fire, yeah. See, there was this supervisor's job he and Ross Barnett were both being considered for, but everybody thought Andrews was going to get it, though Barnett really wanted it and he'd worked for the Forest Service a lot longer plus he had a big degree in forestry, which Andrews didn't, but apparently the bigwigs didn't like him because he was a real bastard to deal with if he didn't like somebody, and some of the guys he didn't like were fair-haired boys of some of the bigwigs.

"Anyway, then Jeff Andrews was killed in the fire and Barnett just stepped right in and started acting like he had the job — you remember all the interviews he gave the newspaper about the fire and all — and then, surprise, surprise, Uncle Jimmy got the job! So Barnett quit in a huff and came up here and started teaching. So how about that for some good gossip?"

"That's what I call good gossip."

The mention of Uncle Jimmy brought his image clearly to mind, the towering man with the craggy face and the rough, deep voice, but with more friendliness behind his eyes than one would at first think. Apparently that friendliness hadn't been there for Whitney as a child, or else she had failed to see it; otherwise she wouldn't have felt so threatened by him. He *was* very big, and to a little girl looking up at him, he must have seemed like a giant, and not a jolly green one. Jolly Green Giant, giant green man, little green men . . . .

Whitney's nightmare had a big man with silver skin in it, didn't it? Or was that not in the dream itself, but something we'd gotten through guided imagery? Could this frightening figure, threatening death, have been Whitney's uncle? Perhaps the dream and the emerging memories associated with it were a kind of collage of things that frightened young Whitney at about the same time in her life — the UFOs, the forest fire with its threat of death, connected with the frightening, giant Uncle Jimmy of the Forest Service . . . .

"Whitney, didn't you say that was your Uncle Jimmy's boat at the river yesterday?"

"Yeah, I guess it's his. I know he used to keep his boat tied up there when I was a kid. I remember him as a big fisherman."

Could Uncle Jimmy have threatened Whitney about going near his boat? She wasn't supposed to be anywhere near the river at all. But suppose he had caught her there and threatened her out of fear for her—certainly it was a dangerous place for an unsupervised little girl to be—and then the place had been destroyed by the fire. She might have blamed herself for the fire because of having disobeyed.

"Do you remember ever getting in trouble for playing around the boat?" I watched Whitney think about this, frowning with concentration. Here I am, I thought, delving into this when even Whitney had agreed it was a matter for discussion at her session next week. I mentally shook my head at myself. Well, I was only collecting information, not opening up the emotional content of the thing. This ought to be all right.

"I seem to have a vague memory of being on the dock when Uncle Jimmy and some other people were taking fish out of the boat. Ugh! I do remember this huge fish he had. It was a river cat, I guess. It was huge! I know it couldn't have been this big, really, but it seems like it was as big as a person, lying there on the dock. I remember myself very small compared to it."

Ah-ha! "In your dream, or your memories about the dream, you saw a dead body."

"Yeah . . . ?"

I waited. I didn't have to wait long. "Oh, T.D.! You think maybe that was that *fish*? And the big man there could have been my uncle? And I was not supposed to be there, because he'd told me not to come down to the river?" Excitement lit up her face. "So the fact that I was being naughty, and then the big dead fish, and Uncle Jimmy—and he could have been wearing coveralls! He did wear them! I remember he wore them! He carried his cigars in the breast pocket and they stuck out the top in a row like little pointed heads covered with cellophane. Wow!''

"So it was silver or gray coveralls, not silver skin?''

"It could have been! Oh, T.D., it could have been!'' She did a little caper on the sidewalk. "Whew! That would explain a lot of it, wouldn't it? I bet that's what all this is about!''

"It may be, Whitney,'' I said, "It well may be.'' The explanation didn't, of course, automatically heal what had obviously been a deep and painful wound, but it would provide a means of beginning to deal with the things in Whitney's childhood which she had found so frightening that she had had to repress them altogether. Now we were ready to make some real progress when we got back into the office setting. I felt a glow of satisfaction.

We came to an intersection of two sidewalks, and Whitney started to turn away from the direction I was headed. We stopped to say a parting word.

"The library's this way,'' she said, and then added with a smile, "but I guess I don't really need to do any more UFO research, do I? If the spaceman was Uncle Jimmy!''

"I suppose not.'' I returned her smile.

"So you're going to meet June?'' she asked, and when I nodded affirmatively, she said, "Well, thank her for me, please. If she hadn't gone on the field trip, I wouldn't have had you all to myself and got this worked out.''

"True.'' And no matter how good it is to have this success with a client, I added silently, it wouldn't compare to spending the weekend with my lover, but one takes what one can get. "And shall I see you next Friday at the usual time?''

"You bet! Oh, wow, I just feel so proud of myself for remembering! — With your help, of course!'' she added.

"You should be. These were hard things for you to remember.''

"Well, anyway, thanks, T.D. Have a good trip home.''

"You, too." I touched her shoulder in congratulation and farewell, and she reached out and touched mine.

We turned to go our separate ways, but before we could take more than a couple of steps, a jolly male voice with an East Texas drawl called, "Hey, Miss Renfro and Miss Way! Y'all got a minute?"

Whitney and I both stopped, turned, and walked back together to meet Ross Barnett.

Our professor had obviously been to church. He looked very different in his Sunday suit than he had the other times we'd seen him. Less like Paul Bunyan and more like an outdoorsy Dan Quayle. "Y'all got a minute?" he repeated as we met. "I got something up at my office I'd like to show you. I think you'll be particularly interested, Whitney."

I looked at my watch. "I have to meet a friend who's on the forestry field trip," I said.

"Oh, no problem," Barnett assured me. "They won't be back for at least another hour, hour and a half yet. Y'all come on up. I want you to see this."

I looked at Whitney, saw that, despite the dislike she'd taken to Barnett yesterday, she was amenable to the idea, and said, "Why not?"

The three of us walked together toward the forestry building.

Chapter 18

As much as I hated to admit it, Barnett appeared to be right about the time of arrival of the field trippers. Not a soul was around the forestry building anywhere that I could see. Since I had no hankering just to sit in the hot car for an hour or more, I was glad of this diversion of his, whatever it might turn out to be.

As we walked, Barnett kept up a stream of good ol' boy small talk, featuring the Lumberjack athletic teams, primarily. One of us must have mentioned that we were from Austin, though I didn't remember doing so, because he referred several times to the University of Texas as being a good enough school, but not up to the standard of this one, particularly when it came to basketball.

"Maybe men's basketball," Whitney said with emphasis, and Barnett visibly checked himself from whatever sexist reply he was about to make, changed it to something innocuous, and dropped the subject. When Whitney, casting about for something to restart the conversation, asked him what he had to show us, he simply grinned and said, "Just you wait and see. I think you'll be surprised."

Whitney and I looked at each other and shrugged our shoulders behind his back.

Barnett opened the glass doors of the forestry building with a key. I supposed there was no reason to leave it open on Sunday, since any studying was probably done in the library — if much studying went on Sunday, anyway. The terrazzo-floored corridor gleamed in the diminished light of a single row of fluorescents, the night lights, I assumed, and gave back hollow, ringing echoes of our steps.

It had been a long time since I had been in a university building as empty as this one was. It brought back bittersweet memories of my college days. I had been in love with a gay boy who worked in the language lab at Texas Tech—this was when I was an undergraduate—and we used to go there late at night sometimes to study together. He had a hard time with math, a subject with which I had no problem. I would help him with his algebra and we would gossip and joke.

He was what I later heard described as a "talk queen," dazzlingly quick-witted, a punster and a sarcastic yet hilarious critic of nearly everything and everyone. I had never known anyone so entertaining. Because he used his facility with words as a shield to deflect the slings and arrows life hurled his way, flashing his intellect instead of flexing his muscles, as it were, I thought he was the most intelligent person I had ever known. I adored him. It came as quite a blow to me when I heard from a third party some of the hilarious, accurate, deep-cutting remarks he made about me. One is often quite tender in one's callow youth.

We followed Barnett up the stairs and down the corridor to his office, where he again produced his key and let us in. I blinked as the bright lights flooded the room; it had been darker in the upstairs corridor than in the ground floor one and it took my eyes a moment to adjust to the light.

"Y'all have a seat," our host told us, turning to open a file drawer. "I just ran across this the other day." We sat; the office was furnished with a pair of serviceable wooden armchairs facing Barnett's desk.

"Here," Barnett said, pulling out a brown envelope and extracting its contents. We got up to see the photograph he laid on the desk.

It was a view of a night skyline. The irregular outline of trees darkened the bottom half of the picture, with the sky slightly lighter in tone above. There were a few faint, short arcs that probably were stars tracking the film in a time exposure. But the most baffling thing in the picture was a bright series of indistinct blobs descending or ascending, one would be hard pressed to tell which, in a slanted series across the sky from one side of the picture to the other.

"What is it?" Whitney asked.

"Well," said Barnett, "much as I hate to admit it, after the hard time I gave you yesterday at lunch, I guess I'd have to say that's a UFO."

Whitney jerked her head up to look at him. He grinned ruefully at her and then at me and said, "Well, I guess sometimes when you don't want to face something, you just get a little too determined to deny it."

"Where did you get this?" said Whitney.

"I took it."

"You took this picture and you still gave me all that bullshit about UFOs coming out of a bottle, or being weather balloons from Palestine?" Whitney cried.

"Now, take it easy!" Barnett, still grinning apologetically, drew back and put up spread hands to ward off her wrath. "Yeah, I took this thing, but, see, I wasn't looking when it happened."

"What do you mean?" Whitney's tone brooked no evasions.

"Well I was taking some pictures of the night sky and the trees, and I set the thing on time exposure and went in the house for something, and I guess whatever that is, there, came by and got its picture took while I was gone. I sure never saw it or anything, but when I developed the film, there that was."

"And so what makes you think it was a UFO?"

"What else could it be?"

Whitney looked at him levelly. "A weather balloon."

"Aw, now . . . !"

"A helicopter. A plane. The planet Venus, the moon, swamp gas."

"Well if it was a plane, it didn't make enough noise for me to hear it in the house with all the windows open. And they don't make lighted weather balloons."

"So how come you were so nasty about it yesterday when I brought up the subject, if you had this mysterious photograph?"

Barnett shrugged and smiled. "Aw, you know how it is. I'd hate to think these things were flying around here, whether they're starting fires or not. And as it happens, this one was right about the same time as the fire we were talking about."

Whitney was exasperated. "So now are you saying you think there might be some chance one of these UFOs *did* start that fire? Well, thanks for your consideration. You realize you made me feel like an idiot for even suggesting that? And now your conscience gets the better of you, probably because you went to church, and you bring this picture out and everything's supposed to be all right?"

"I know I was out of line yesterday. No kidding, I really do. But can't you see it from my point of view? See, I was pretty upset about that particular fire when it happened. You know I lost a friend in there. I spent a long time trying to get to understand how that all could have happened." He cast an appealing look at me. "You know what I'm talking about, don't you, Dr. Renfro? It takes a while to get used to the idea that something so meaningless could just snuff out a life like it didn't count for a thing."

"It is hard to face," I agreed.

"It is. So anyway, Whitney, I was a little rough on you yesterday because I just didn't like thinking, on top of how meaningless it all seemed at the time and still does, that it could have possibly been caused by something I could never in this world understand. I mean, a lightning strike or a careless smoker I could handle, but to think some kind of flying saucer did that? Heck, no! I just have a durn hard time with that idea."

"So what did make you change your mind?" Whitney wasn't going to be placated easily. I could see she was still holding serious reservations about Barnett and his motives. I had some, too but for different reasons. I was almost positive he hadn't known I was Dr. Renfro yesterday. I wondered whom he had been talking to. Whitney certainly hadn't told anybody in my hearing that I was her therapist, or even what my profession was. He must have found out by some chance. And possibly even that could be a factor in his new openness about the UFO. It might not be that he was trying to make things up with Whitney so much as with me, after all his talk about craziness and his superiority in dealing with people. He must have felt chagrined when he found out who I was.

Whether it was because of me or Whitney that he felt obliged to take this new stance, it was certainly Whitney whom he was now trying his best to appease. She hadn't yielded with grace on the issues as he had doubtless hoped she would. I, myself, was enjoying watching her feisty response.

"I didn't really know you were personally concerned, yesterday. You just told me you were interested in the fire historically," Barnett answered her. "I should have realized that your woods that you used to play in were involved, since I knew who your folks were and all. I guess I was still just thinking about you as another college kid, not as somebody who really cared what had happened."

"And how did you find out otherwise?" Whitney wanted to know.

"I saw ol' Bob, your cousin, at church this morning and we got to talking, that's all."

A blush began to creep up Whitney's neck. "And what did he tell you?"

"Oh, just that you were talking about playing in the woods as a kid and how you were worried you might have had something to do with starting the fire, that's all."

"He told you that?"

"And that you were looking into the UFO angle because of some dream you'd had." Seeing the blood suffusing her face, he continued quickly, "Listen, I can understand exactly how you'd feel. I have nightmares about fires myself, too, sometimes, and they're part of my stock in trade."

Whitney, speechless at this betrayal of her confidences by her cousin, simply stared at him.

Casting about for something to patch the inadvertent damage he was doing his cause, Barnett said, "Look, if you're interested, I've got some more pictures you haven't seen yet. Some views of the river, the way it used to look—" He rummaged in his file drawer and quickly spilled a small sheaf of black and white photos across the desk top. "Here. Here's a hunting camp from back when you were probably a baby, and here's some guys that got a good day's catch in the old Angelina . . . ."

"What's this?" Whitney was looking at a picture she had pulled from under the stack. I moved over to look at it. It showed a man in something that looked like an aluminized beekeeper's suit, but without a bee veil.

"That? Oh, that was an experimental firefighting suit. Supposed to keep front line firefighters from burning up. Worked okay, but it was expensive and clumsy. Don't use that kind now."

He reached to take the picture from her hand, but they missed the connection somehow and it fell to the floor. Whitney quickly knelt to pick it up, Barnett stooping also, but a little slower to react than she. Retrieving the photograph, Whitney looked up at Barnett bending over her, stopped moving, looked down at the picture in her hand, then up once more at the man who stood waiting with his hand out.

"Oh, God," she said softly. The blood visibly drained from her face.

"Need a hand?" Barnett said amiably, grinning and stretching his out to her.

Whitney, pale as death, jerked back from the proffered assistance like a frightened animal.

"What is it, Whitney?" I said, moving to her. She lurched to her feet and took what looked like an involuntary step backward.

"Nothing. Just a little dizzy. Too much beer last night, I guess." She produced a ghastly grin. "Sorry. I think I'd better get out in the fresh air. Mr. Barnett, thanks for showing us your pictures."

Barnett was looking at her hard, his head cocked and his brows pulled into a hard-thinking frown.

"I'll walk you to your car," he said slowly. "You don't want to faint on us or anything."

"No, thanks! Really, I'll be fine. T.D., let's go."

She turned and started for the door, but Barnett, to my surprise, moved in front of her and caught her gently by the upper arms. "Now, don't you think you ought to sit down a minute until you feel better? Put your head between your knees?" He pushed her toward a chair, but she suddenly struggled and broke his hold on her.

"Let me go!" The scream had a hysterical note in it.

Barnett crossed the distance between himself and the office door in one stride and slammed it closed. The smile was still locked on his face, but obviously it wasn't a smile any more. "I think you'd better just sit a while, Whitney. You, too, Dr. Renfro, why don't you? I see something's bothering Whitney, and I think she ought to tell me what it is."

"You know damn well what it is!" Whitney cried. "UFO, my foot! I remember, T.D. I remembered it just now, when I saw the picture and then him standing there like that."

"What did you remember, Whitney?" I said, keeping a calm tone. "What is it?"

"The man with the silver skin. It wasn't my uncle with a fish, it was what I thought it was all along."

Barnett leaned against the edge of his desk, watching us.

"We need to talk about this in therapy, T.D. Really, it explains a lot of my old fears, and," she looked at Barnett—"I can't go into it now. Let's just go."

"Mr. Barnett," I said, rising, "this really is a matter for a private session. So excuse us, please, and thank you for your help—"

Barnett said, "I don't think you'd better leave yet, doctor. Whitney, tell me what you think you remember."

"Nothing. Nothing that concerns you."

"I think it does."

I took Whitney's arm and we both got up and moved toward the door, but Barnett slipped in front of us, holding up a tan and calloused hand.

"Mr. Barnett, please move aside now and let us go," I said in a firmly assertive tone. I was not quite sure what was happening here, but it was clear we were virtually being held in the office against our wills. I took a half-step forward and Barnett placed his palm against my chest and with no evident effort shoved me off balance so that I almost fell.

"You started that fire, Whitney." His voice was low and emphatic. "You started it, you and your little campfire. Oh, yeah, I can save you a therapy bill on that one. You don't have to dredge up the details from your subconscious, Whitney, because I can tell you all about it. You started that fire, and I know it because I saw you there. I didn't want you to feel too bad, so I went along with your UFO idea today, but sweetheart, you started it. I saw you running off when Jeff and I came by in the jeep."

"No. I don't believe you!"

"You'd better believe me, because it's true."

"No, it isn't." She looked at him, then looked wildly at the door and at me. "Or maybe it is. Okay, I guess it is. I do remember now. I started it." She was talking fast now. "I was playing Indians in the woods. I had a campfire. The wind got it, and I ran away. T.D., we need to talk about this, but right now all I want is not to think about it."

She stood up and made a dash for the door, I started to follow, and Barnett, who had been listening without comment, put his hand on the doorknob and held it fast.

"I believe you do remember, kid. But I don't believe you remember what you say you did. Now before you go, you tell me what you really remember, or think you do."

"I remember the fire!"

"And you remember that Jeff got out of the jeep and chased you?"

"Yes! I remember he chased me, yes."

Barnett shook his head. "No you don't."

"Yes, I do! I remember that!"

"No, because it didn't happen. None of that happened, and you know it. Now level with me, because you're not leaving this office until you do."

"Mr. Barnett," I said, "whatever happened is over. Nothing is going to change it. Wouldn't it be better to think about this for a while, and then we can talk later?"

"It's too late already, doctor. Now, come on girl, get it over with. You're lying, and I need to know what you think you saw. And you'll tell me, unless you want to stay here all day, you and your shrink who wants to meet her girlfriend and go home, I'll betcha." He managed a tremulous smile. "Now, please. You know I've got to deal with this, now don't you?"

Whitney didn't answer.

"Come on, Whitney. I know about what you must have seen, and I can handle it okay, but I need to hear it from you, don't you see? I've lived with it long enough, but before I can do anything about it, I really need to hear it from somebody who was there. It's been a long time, and memory gets confused . . . . Now what do you say? Please? And then y'all can go home, okay?"

Whitney looked at me hopelessly, then turned to Barnett. "I remember the silver suit. You know that."

Barnett sighed. "Yeah. I know that. And Andrews? You remember Andrews, too?"

"I remember, if that's who that was."

"It was."

"What do you remember about Andrews?"

"I remember him . . . lying on the ground."

Barnett nodded. "And what else?"

"I don't . . . ."

"It's okay. You can say it. I'm not going to hurt you or anything stupid like that; not now, after all these years of living with it." He sighed. "I guess I'm ready to face up to it. It would just help to hear it from somebody who was there, that's all. Tell me what else you remember, won't you?"

Whitney looked from Barnett to me, then said, "I remember a man in a silver suit pouring something out of a can. And then there was fire everywhere, and I was afraid I was going to die, like the man on the ground. Like Andrews."

Sadly, Barnett shook his head. "I never even knew you were there, girl. I had no idea, until I heard about that dream of yours this morning. Your cousin Bob ought to keep a confidence better, I guess. But I knew it, then. It had to be." He fell silent for a moment, his eyes looking far away. "All these years there was a witness, waiting like a time bomb." He sighed again, and again he shook his head. "And I didn't even get the job. Even after Jeff was dead, I didn't get the job."

Whitney and I kept quiet.

"Well." Barnett brought himself back to the present with a slight jerk. "So now what, ladies?"

"Now you must decide, Mr. Barnett," I said. "You can either own up to what happened, or you can refuse to deal with it. It's up to you."

"But not entirely up to me, is it?"

Neither Whitney nor I spoke.

"Because I can't see you two just keeping this to yourselves."

"We probably all need time to think," I said.

"Yeah. We do." He paused, then continued. "So, you see that door over there?"

He gestured to the wall opposite his desk, behind the chairs where we'd been sitting. There was a door, solid metal, like the other interior doors in the building, painted gray to match the rest of the trim. "I'd appreciate it if y'all would just step in there for a few minutes where I'll know you're safe, while I think about all this. It's a closet, but there's room to sit on the floor, if you're friendly."

"You're going to lock us in there?" Whitney asked on a rising note of panic.

"Now, it won't be for long. Just until I decide what to do. Please, go on. Don't make me hurt you."

"Ross," I said gently, "You're feeling frightened now, but I don't think you really want to do anything else you'll regret. I really think it might help if you talked about it."

"Just leave me alone, will you?" His voice was suddenly loud, the plea in it overlaid with anger. "Now get in that closet! I told you I need to think, and I mean it. Now get in there!"

"This has been a shock to you, Ross—"

"Move!"

He didn't have a weapon, and there were two of us. But he was stronger than Whitney and I put together, and we knew it, and he was desperate; we now realized that, also. We opened the door and walked into the closet.

"Give me your purse, Dr. Renfro," Barnett said. "I'll need to borrow your car for a while." He reached out and took my purse out of my hand. "I'll be back," he said.

"Ross, you don't need to lock us up—" I reasoned, urgency showing through in my tone despite the effort I was making to keep my voice soothing.

The door closed, and a key turned in the lock.

Chapter 19

We heard the click of the light switch in the office, and then the closing of the outer door.

"Oh, damn, T.D.," Whitney said, and groped for my hand. Her own was shaking. I moved to put my arms around her, and she clung to me, shuddering, holding tight, and I must say the clinging was not all on her side. I was more than slightly shaken, myself.

After a few moments she managed a little laugh and said, "And I thought I would never go back in the closet!"

"Oh, Whitney, really!" I said, and we burst into brief, hysterical giggles.

When we'd stopped, I took a deep breath, feeling Whitney do the same, and with an effort we relaxed our death grip on each other and started to assess the situation.

We were in almost total darkness, the only light coming faintly from a crack under the door. This was a narrow space about an inch high. At least it ought to let in some air. Not, I hoped, that we were going to be here long enough for air to become a problem. Since Barnett had turned off the light in the office, what filtered in from outside didn't do much to show us our surroundings.

"God, what do we do?" Whitney's voice was small.

"Let's see if there's an inside latch on the door." I felt along the edge of the door and found, as I had hoped, a small revolving catch which should open the bolt. "Eureka!" I said, but my satisfaction was short-lived. The catch spun freely under my fingers. "It's broken."

Whitney tried it, too, and gave up with a frustrated whimper.

"Let's find out about where we are, anyway," I said, sounding more businesslike than I felt. "You feel around on your side and I'll do the same over here." We did that, groping in the dark.

"You have anything interesting?" Whitney asked, and I replied, "Probably copies of exams or something. Just papers in stacks."

"Stick some under your shirt," she advised. "If they're exams, we can sell them to students next semester."

"I certainly hope we won't be here next semester!"

We giggled, but there was a sharp note of anxiety in it.

"There's a coat or something here," Whitney said, "hanging on a hook. That's about all."

"Here's something." My hand had fallen on what I instantly recognized as a pair of scissors. "For whatever good these might do us," I said, telling Whitney about them.

She felt them in my hand and said, "Give them to me. Maybe we can get the door open."

I handed them over, and we sidled around each other to give her access to the lock. She worked for some time, grunting now and then with the effort. "I'm trying to get the blade wedged into the frame," she explained, "but I can't ... quite ... get .... Damn!" The scissors slipped with a metallic scrape. "I almost had it." Doggedly she set to work again.

In the end she gave it up. The door fit too tightly. It had been a forlorn hope, anyway, but at least it had passed some time.

How much time, we didn't know. I wished I had an ugly plastic sports watch like those June favored, because I recalled hers had a light in it. "Can you see your watch?" I asked Whitney.

"I'll try." She got down on the floor by the bottom of the door and, after a few moments of contortions, said, "Maybe if I take it off ...." This worked. She held her watch on the floor in the sliver of light and, pressing her face close to it, announced, "One-fifteen."

One fifteen. June's group ought to be back by now. Or soon, anyway. I said this to Whitney.

"Do you think they'll come up here?"

"I don't know."

"Maybe they will."

I didn't see why they would, but I saw no reason to throw cold water on this hopeful idea. I said, "Maybe they will."

Whitney stayed on the floor, and after a minute I said, "We might as well get comfortable."

"Might as well; can't dance," Whitney agreed.

I lowered myself into the remaining floor space with an effort. There really was not much room for two people to sit there. "Good thing we're friendly," I said, thinking of Barnett's remark.

"Isn't it!"

The floor was hard. We sat and shifted, trying to find positions that didn't cramp or rub our bones too hard on the unyielding surface, and then Whitney had the brilliant idea of getting down the coat that she'd found hanging in the wall and sitting on that. I got up again and got it, we arranged it under us, and, after experimenting a while, we achieved a marginal degree of comfort, sitting close, leaning against one wall with our knees drawn up and our feet touching the other side of the closet.

"I gather," I said when we were settled, "that Barnett killed Jeff Andrews and set fire to his body?" I shuddered inwardly at the enormity of the idea.

"I guess so. Damn it, T.D., if only I hadn't let on!"

"He didn't give you much choice, Whitney. And he sounded sincere about facing up to it."

"I don't mean at the last. I mean, I shouldn't have acted like I remembered anything in the first place. He'd never have known. We'd be out of here."

"Maybe. But I don't think he brought us over here just to show us his flying saucer. I think he was fishing to find out what you knew. It might have come out the same, anyway."

"But I had to let him know I knew! Oh, *hell!* And I'm going to *kill* Bob! Why did I have to tell him all that? God, T.D., I feel so stupid!"

"You trusted someone you used to be close to, and he made a bad judgment about telling someone else. You had no way of knowing he'd do that."

"I shouldn't have drunk his damn beer."

"You were enjoying yourself with your cousin. There's nothing wrong with that."

"And I had to drag you into it. Hell, I told him all about you, and about June, and about being in therapy —I betrayed your confidence, T.D."

"Whitney, there was nothing confidential to betray. My profession and my lover aren't secrets, you know."

"But you trusted me . . . ."

"Whitney. There is nothing wrong with talking about your life and your friends with someone you trust. If I tell you something I don't want you to repeat, I'll let you know. But it was yourself you were really talking about to Bob, not me and June. Now give yourself a break!"

She sighed. "I know, I know. But I still hate myself for doing it. Okay!" she hastened to forestall me, "what I mean is, I regret that this has happened."

"You feel—?"

"I feel . . . that if you're going to bill me for all this, which you certainly have a right to, I'm going to have to get a second job! I'm shutting up about it now. Want me to look at my watch again, so you can keep count of what I owe you?"

"That won't be necessary. You're on the daily rate, now!" I patted her on the knee, and she placed her hand over mine.

Silence fell. I thought about June getting off her bus and looking around for me and the Mustang. Barnett presumably had moved my car so she wouldn't see it there. That was the only reason I could think of for his taking my purse and keys. He must surely have transportation of his own, if transportation was all he needed. And he had said he would be back soon. He must have just gone down to move my car to someplace where June wouldn't see it, so she would think I was somewhere other than in the immediate vicinity. That way there would be less chance she would come looking for me here.

I mentioned this to Whitney.

"And after he throws off pursuit, what is he going to do?" she asked.

It was not something I cared to think about, but on the other hand, it was the one question burning in both of our minds. "One hesitates to speculate," I admitted.

"One hesitates, but one does it, anyway. Oh, God, T.D., this guy's murdered a man. What's he going to do with us?"

I had been keeping that thought away, but her voicing it made it undeniable. What, indeed, would Barnett think he could do at this point? He had a witness to the original crime. How much water her testimony would hold after all these years, I couldn't say. But at the very least, it ought to reopen the inquiry. And of course that wasn't the only evidence against him any more, because Whitney and I had both heard what amounted to his confession and his statement of motive: he had killed Jeff Andrews to get his job.

"He did talk much of the time like he was ready to face what he did and its consequences," I said.

"But he also compounded the felony by locking us up and taking your car."

Again, we were silent.

"He must have wanted that job badly," I said.

"It doesn't seem like much of a reason for killing somebody."

"No, it doesn't."

"I guess he kills without too much reason, huh?"

"He seems to have, at least that time."

"He has a better reason to kill us."

She was right about that. He might kill us to keep from being arrested for murder. "But he's older now," I said. "Older than he looks, too. He must be in his mid-forties, at least."

"He doesn't show it. He looks about thirty-five."

"Let's hope he's learned by now that brute force doesn't get him what he wants."

"Let's hope so." She crowded tighter against me, turning her face inward against my shoulder, and I put my arm around her and felt her firm, young body pressing against mine like that of a frightened child.

"It wouldn't be the smartest thing in the world to try to get rid of us," I said.

Whitney didn't answer.

"It may be that he'll think better of all this and just let us go."

"How could he?"

"It would be the smart thing to do. He can't really hope to get away now."

"He might run for it."

"He might do that. He could get a head start today, and be out of state, at least, before anybody knows he's gone."

"It's not far to Louisiana," Whitney agreed, shifting and sitting up to ease her cramped position. "When all the counties around here were dry, people used to run over to Shreveport to buy liquor. The state line's not forty miles. He could even get there by boat, across Sam Rayburn Reservoir."

"He might try a getaway."

"God, if he does, that means we'll be here all night!"

"Oh, god." All night, at least. Who knew when somebody might come close enough for us to attract attention? We were in a locked closet in a locked office, of which Barnett presumably had the only key, unless a janitor happened by. "I wonder what's on the other side of this wall?" I said. "Maybe somebody in the next office would hear us if we banged on the wall."

"Nobody will be there now, though."

"Unless somebody comes up after the field trip," I offered hopefully.

"I haven't heard a thing."

"Neither have I, but let's try, anyway." I stood up stiffly and hammered on the back wall of the closet with my fist. It hurt, and the noise didn't seem very loud. The wall must be quite solid. Whitney joined me, and we banged away in unison, stopping to listen every few blows. Nothing.

We shifted our attack and banged on the door. If someone was passing in the corridor, we might make enough noise that way to attract attention. The door made more noise than the wall had, but not much. Then we tried the side walls. One of these was obviously the outside wall of the building, and we left that after a few experimental knocks confirmed its thickness, but the other made a satisfyingly hollow sound. "Maybe it's the closet in the other office," I speculated.

We beat the wall until our fists were sore, but no sound answered us. At length we gave up and sat down again.

"What will June do when you don't show up?" Whitney asked after a while.

"I don't know. Go back to the motel, I suppose. After that, I have no idea."

June would be irritated that I hadn't shown up to meet her. But when I wasn't at the motel, either, she would start to worry. Poor June, not knowing even where to begin to look for me. She would know I wouldn't abandon her, and all our things would still be in our room. I thought of the bed with the smooth sheets, neatly made up and awaiting the joyfully reunited lovers. I could see in my imagination June pacing the room, going to the phone and then not knowing whom to call, pacing some more, looking out the door to see if my Mustang was at last turning into the parking lot. Would she call the police eventually? After how long? Oh, June, honey, call quickly, call now!

"Is anyone expecting you at a certain time?" I asked Whitney hopefully.

"Not really. I said good-bye to my folks this morning. I thought I'd just do a little quick look through the card catalog at the library here and then head on back for Austin."

"Nobody's expecting you in Austin?"

"Marilyn, but not at any special time, though I told her I'd be back today or tonight. I imagine she's already worried. But she knows she's a worrier, so she won't try to do anything about it. Not tonight, anyway."

"You don't think she'd call your mother to find out if you've left?"

"Marilyn doesn't feel too comfortable with my mother."

"So I recall."

June, call somebody! Call the police; call the hospital. Start them looking for my car. June, honey, help me!

"I wish this closet had a bathroom," Whitney said.

"Oh, don't talk about it!"

"Maybe he'll hurry up."

He didn't hurry. Time became meaningless. We waited in the dark.

"It was nasty of him to try to pin the fire on you like that."

"And stupid. That's when I knew I was right about the other—the body."

I didn't want to think about the body. "He could have at least thrown us a sandwich," I said.

"And the Sunday paper and a flashlight."

"No kidding."

"A radio would be nice, too."

Silence.

"We could sing," I suggested.

"Do you know 'Come Out of the Closet'? Maxine Feldman sings it."

"No, but it sounds appropriate! Sing it for me."

She began singing softly. It was a gay liberation song. I found the lines, "Come out of the closet/Be free," particularly poignant, given our situation. Also the line, "I know it's dark in there."

"Hell!" Whitney broke off the song and abruptly struggled to her feet. "Help me, T.D. I'm going to break through this wall."

She attacked the one hollow-sounding wall with her foot, kicking hard with the heel of her shoe. Unfortunately she had on athletic shoes, less effective as tools for the purpose than boots would have been. I kicked, too.

And gradually I thought I felt the sheetrock begin to give. A few more kicks and I knew it was true; my foot was definitely making a dent in the material of the wall.

"Getting somewhere!" grunted Whitney, crashing her foot into the wall with vicious force to punctuate her words. "God . . . damn it . . . T.D., . . . I think . . . we're . . . .GET-TING it!"

I heard a crunching sound, and Whitney cried, "My foot's through!" She stopped kicking and stood panting, leaning with me against the opposite wall.

"Let's see where we are," she said when she got her breath. I heard her ripping at the sheetrock in the dark, and I joined her, feeling tho hole growing beneath my fingers, little by little.

"I can't see anything through there," I said.

"There'll be another layer of sheetrock to get through on the other side of the wall. Let's open this one up and then try to poke a hole with the scissors."

Whitney wasn't the worst person to be imprisoned with, I was finding out. I certainly couldn't have imagined myself doing this demolition job alone.

We worked on. I felt the grit of the sheetrock packing painfully under my nails; the dust filled my nostrils with a dry, slightly acrid odor, and I imagined I could feel it caking the sweat on my arms and face. I ignored it and went on ripping, and soon we had a hole that felt several inches across.

"Now let me make a hole in the other side and see what we can see," Whitney said. I stood back and rested while she groped for the scissors, found them, and dug at the wall again.

"Ha!"

"Did you get it?"

"Yeah. Let me just enlarge this . . . . Hmm." I stood with my hand on her back as she bent to put her eye near the hole she had made. "No light," she reported, "but at least there's nothing huge and immovable against the other side of the wall right here. Come on, T.D. Let's get this hole big enough to squeeze through. If it's a closet, I'll bet it won't be locked. And even if it is, it'll at least give us another room to our prison!"

"Right!"

Working side by side, resting now and then, we doggedly plugged away at our task. It was slower work than one would think. The sheetrock in this building was made of stern stuff. Whitney said we'd have done better with a hammer, but Barnett had thoughtlessly neglected to provide us with one.

"Slow going," she said at one point.

"But it's going," I said. "We're making progress."

"Beats waiting."

It did beat waiting.

It took roughly two hours to get the hole through both sides of the wall large enough for me, the smaller of us, to squeeze painfully through. Whitney looked at her watch now and then by the light coming under the door. But at last I thought I could try the escape route, and, with Whitney pushing and unsnagging my clothes as necessary, I wriggled through into the space beyond.

It was a closet or storage room, and we'd been lucky in our choice of location for our hole in the wall. It seemed to be the only place where there was any room at all, a narrow cranny with just standing room for one. The rest of the space seemed to be filled with what felt like cardboard boxes, heavily packed. I stretched up as far as I could without quite reaching the top of the stacks, and I could find no sign of the door. To get to it, we would have to shift a formidable amount of stuff.

I reported this to Whitney, and she said, "Will any of the boxes fit through our hole?"

I measured with my hands as best I could. It didn't look hopeful. I could see what she was driving at, and she outlined the idea for me as I thought about it. It would be more possible to shift the stacks of boxes if we could move some of them into our closet.

"And it's a good bet that when we get to the door over there, the lock will work from the inside the way it's supposed to, and we'll be out of here," she concluded.

"Let's go," I said. We set to work with a will.

Chapter 20

In the narrow confines of our closet cell the heat, bearable when we sat still, rose to extremely uncomfortable levels as we exerted ourselves. I felt grimy, sticky, and tired, but I knew Whitney did, too, and she wasn't complaining. We stuck to our task, and eventually we had the sheetrock removed entirely from between two wall studs from near floor level to a height that would let me squeeze through while stooping only slightly.

Once I was through the opening, I had the formidable job of wrestling the heavy cartons out of their stacks and passing them to Whitney. They would fit through the opening we had made only with the greatest difficulty, and I mashed my fingers more than once.

When we had laboriously shifted three of the boxes, I was able to climb up where they had been and reach over the remaining ones to find the door which we hoped would lead us to freedom.

"Can you feel anything?" Whitney asked, listening to me scrabble for purchase on the smooth cardboard.

"No." To my dismay, I found at least one more rank of boxes, and maybe more. The storage room must be more than a closet. There was no telling how big it was, or even which way to go to find the door. The room must be packed solid.

I reported this discouraging news to Whitney.

"Come out and rest a minute and let's think about this," she said.

I did that gratefully.

There was even less floor space now that the three hard-won boxes from the other room were with us, but the fact that we now had a place to sit besides the floor more than compensated for that. We sat on the boxes, leaned back in relative comfort against the wall, and relaxed for a few minutes.

Tiredness wilted my resolve to go on with what seemed a futile attempt at freedom. My mashed fingers bothered me, now that the logistics of box-moving weren't claiming all my attention. I sat massaging them gingerly in the dark.

"You think we can get out that way?" Whitney asked.

I thought about it. The number of boxes we'd have to shift, the fact that we didn't know the size or layout of the room, the additional fact that I was already tired and I knew Whitney must be, too, these things combined to discourage any further efforts. On the other hand, what other alternative did we have?

"To wait for Barnett to come back and do whatever he decides to do," Whitney said.

"He might just let us go."

"He might just knock us in the head and put us down the incinerator, too."

I didn't reply.

"Or he might be on his way to Mexico by now, and nobody will find us until who knows when."

True. Oh, June, June, somebody, help!

"Let's get back to work," I said.

And really, the problem wasn't as impossible to solve as I had at first thought. If I could get a couple more boxes out to Whitney, I could then shift the neighboring stack sideways and, climbing into the resulting space, explore again with my hands for a clue to the direction I ought to be moving. Learning the layout of the storage room was like working one of those puzzles where a block can only move into the space left by moving another. It was not going to be impossible, though it would doubtless take some time. I explained this to Whitney, who said, "Great! Time, we've got!"

Or did we? The more I thought about Barnett, the more it seemed to me that he might come back at any moment, and the more desirable it seemed to me that he find his caged birds flown. I redoubled my efforts.

Each time I would get a stack of boxes shifted to open a new avenue of exploration, I would climb hopefully into the space I had made and feel as far as my arms could reach, hoping for contact with a wall or a door. But after three hard-won tries, I was worn out and more discouraged than ever. I crawled back into our closet and collapsed onto the makeshift seat.

"If I could just get up on top of the damned things and crawl around until I find the door," I complained, "things would be a lot simpler."

"But you can't?"

"There's just not quite room. The damned things are stacked right to the ceiling."

"Shit."

"Try not to mention bodily functions, Whitney, in the absence of appropriate facilities."

"Sorry," she said, and added, "I'll be glad to get out of here for more reasons than one."

"No shit," I agreed.

"Exactly."

We sat silent for a while. I wondered what time it was. When Whitney checked her watch by the light under the door, she said, "Hell, T.D., it's nearly six o'clock!"

"Time flies when you're having fun."

"Isn't that bastard ever going to come back? Where the hell *is* he?"

"I don't know." June, oh, June, come and open the door and scoop me up and take me home! I want a hot bath with bubbles that smell like spring flowers, and a soft towel to rub me dry and my sweet lover to tuck me in bed and stroke my hair and sing me to sleep in her arms.

"Let me go in there this time," Whitney said, jogging me out of my reverie. "You stay here and rest a while."

"Do you think there's room for you in there? It's pretty cramped."

"We'll see." She got up, and I heard her grunting and muttering as she wedged herself through the opening and into the room beyond. I pulled my feet up and curled into the corner.

I have always had the capacity to doze off in the presence of stress. I slipped into vague dreams, jerking myself out now and then as Whitney bumped about in the storage room, but always sliding back, deeper and deeper until I knew no more.

I awoke as Whitney was sitting down beside me.

"Are you asleep?" she was asking.

"I think so. I didn't mean to conk out on you."

"I'm about to give up," she said. "No, you don't have to move. Here, you can curl up against me. Now, here's what I thought. Suppose we stack up the boxes we have in here and a couple more in front of the door. Then when he comes and opens the door, we can push the stack over on him and get out. What do you think?"

I thought that by this time Barnett wasn't coming back, but I hesitated to say it yet. Obviously he had done more than just think about things for the few minutes he'd promised when he locked us in. If he came back now to get us, Whitney's worst fears might prove true, that he was coming to dispose of two dangerous witnesses against him.

"Let's do it," I said, straightening cramped legs and getting up.

The stack, when we finished it, was precariously balanced. A strong push would send it toppling outward with enough force, we hoped, to bring down whomever opened the door. Surely if it were anyone but Barnett, he or she would call us or make some kind of sound that would keep us from knocking our rescuer silly.

Spoiled by the luxury of our box seats, we also wrestled two more of the cartons into our space so we could sit in relative comfort while we waited. The light from the

crack under the door, now partially obscured by the booby
trap we had constructed for our captor, was fading fast.
Night was coming, and so far rescue was not.

"June must be frantic by now," Whitney said.

"Yes, she must."

"Maybe she's already called the cops."

"Surely she has."

"It can't be long, now."

We shifted, resettled, and composed ourselves to wait.

I slept again. Whitney did, too; when I half awoke
some time later, she was breathing evenly, slumped against
my shoulder.

What woke me? Something, I thought. A noise? I listened intently. Nothing . . . . But wait! The light coming
under the door was brighter. Daylight? No. We couldn't
have slept that long. The light in the office was on!

I shook Whitney cautiously so as not to startle her
into making a sound. "Whitney, wake up! I think he's back."

"Wha . . . ?"

"Shh! I think he's back. There's light under the door."

I felt her sit up quickly. "Can you hear him?" she
whispered.

"No."

"It could be somebody else."

"If it is, they won't know we're in here."

"Unless we tell them!"

Simultaneously we started yelling "Help!" and bang-
ing on the walls and the boxes as if our lives depended
on it, which, as far as we knew, they might.

No glad, responsive cry answered us, but now there
was a jingle of keys outside, and the shadow of a foot at
the bottom of the door. Not much doubt this was Barnett.

We stopped yelling.

"It's him. Get ready!" Whitney whispered.

We poised ourselves with hands on the stacked boxes
as the key scraped at the lock, the bolt clicked back, and
the door started to open. As the blinding light flooded
our prison, Whitney yelled, "Now!" We shoved the boxes
for all we were worth.

I got a glimpse of Barnett's startled face as the towering stack overbalanced and toppled toward him. There was a rumbling crash and an angry cry, and Whitney was shouting, "Run! Run!"

We scrambled over the boxes, but Barnett wasn't down as we had hoped he would be. He had merely sidestepped and flattened himself against the open door, and now he said, "Not so fast!" as he stepped between us and the door of the office, and Whitney, starting back, stumbled over a box and fell, crying out as her ankle twisted.

I stood still, facing Barnett. I wanted to make eye contact with him and face him down, but I had unusual difficulty in doing that, for my gaze seemed involuntarily rivetted to the round, dark hole in the end of the barrel of the huge, blue-black revolver pointing steadily at my heart.

Chapter 21

Ross Barnett didn't look like a ruffian or a steely-eyed killer. He had changed clothes from his suit into jeans and a sport shirt, both nicely pressed, and the lace-up boots on his feet looked oiled and well-cared for. He looked the part of the open-faced outdoorsman, a little apologetic, actually, as he moved the gun barrel in a short gesture that took in Whitney as well as me and said, "Both of you stand over by the wall."

"Are you all right?" I asked Whitney, taking a step toward her. She had fallen hard, and her mouth was bleeding slightly.

"Get over there, T.D. She can take care of herself." Barnett flicked the gun barrel in the direction he wanted me to go.

I stopped. "Ross," I said, "take it easy. We're not fools. We're going to do what you want, but Whitney's hurt. Can't you see that?"

Whitney, who had struggled to a sitting position, said, "I'm okay." But when she started to get to her feet, her ankle gave and she cried out in pain. I knelt beside her before Barnett could object.

"It's swelling already," I told him, looking up at the gun and then forcing my eyes upward to his. "We need to get ice on it and get it bandaged. Is there any ice in the building, Ross? A refrigerator or an ice machine? How about the faculty lounge?"

"There's a refrigerator down in the—hell, no you don't!" He scowled. "Don't try any funny business on me,

Miss Headshrinker. Just get her up and get over there by that wall like I told you, and don't talk."

"She can't walk on that, Ross. Whitney, can you walk, do you think?" She shook her head. Her eyes, as mine had been, were locked onto the gun, and tears were starting down her cheeks. Cry, Whitney, cry! I thought. Bring out every chivalrous instinct he has in him. Aloud I said, "Help me get her to a chair."

I slipped an arm around Whitney's shoulders and started to lift, and she helped as much as she could. We nearly fell, nevertheless, and Barnett almost involuntarily caught her arm and guided her to a chair, but without putting down his gun, unfortunately. I pulled the other chair over and lifted the injured ankle onto it. "Ross," I commanded our captor, "please get that coat out of the closet so I can use it for a pillow here. This needs to be elevated."

Barnett backed toward the closet, still pointing his gun in our direction. I hoped he might trip over the boxes on the floor and fall, but he was careful. He got the coat, which I saw in the light was a nice buffalo plaid jacket, wrinkled now from our sitting on it, and I rolled it up and placed it under Whitney's ankle.

"How is it?" I asked her.

"It hurts."

"How's your mouth? Let me take a look." Her teeth had cut her lip when she fell, but it didn't look serious. "We need some water and a cloth to get this cleaned up," I told Barnett.

"Look," he said. "This is all very touching, your concern for your buddy, but it really doesn't matter, does it?"

"Of course it matters. The woman's in pain!"

"She can walk if she tries. We're all going to walk out of here, so come on. You've fooled around enough."

"Walk?" I put all my indignation into the word. "She can't walk! She needs an elastic bandage and a cane, at least, and it really ought to be X-rayed. She might even need a cast on it. Now, use the good sense God gave you and help me get her to a doctor. That mouth injury looks bad, as well.''

''There's no way she's going to see any doctor, lady!''

''Well, if you won't help her, I will!'' I started purposefully toward the door, and for a second or two I thought I was going to get away with it.

''Now, just wait one minute!'' Barnett said. I reached the door and was extending my hand toward the knob, when I felt a more powerful hand than mine grip my shoulder and jerk me almost off my feet. He shoved me hard toward Whitney and the chairs, and I barely caught myself by grabbing the edge of the desk to keep from landing in Whitney's lap.

''Get her up!''

''She can't—''

''Get her up! Now! Get up, girl!'' He waved the gun wildly. ''I'm not kidding. On your feet, both of you. You're going to walk out of here and you're going to do it now, and if I hear one peep out of either one of you, I'll brain you, and I'm not kidding one little bit. So move.''

''You can't seriously think—''

The gun barrel came down on my shoulder in a vicious blow that turned my words into a screech.

''T.D.!'' cried Whitney, and Barnett repeated, ''Move!''

We moved. Whitney leaned on me and hobbled, barely able to touch her foot to the floor, and Barnett followed us closely. I couldn't see the gun, but I could almost feel its barrel boring into the small of my back.

''Open the door.''

I opened it. We struggled into the corridor, very dark now, with only the exit light next to the stairs to illuminate the emptiness. Barnett clicked off the office light behind us and closed the door.

''You bitches really fucked up my closet, didn't you?'' he said.

''Surely you can't blame us for trying to get out. It's what you would have done yourself, Ross.'' Talk, Ross, argue, discuss. Come, let us reason together.

"Shut up and walk." The gun jabbed me in the back-
bone.

"Look," I tried again. "You've had us locked up for
hours. At least let us go to the restroom. If we have to
wait much longer, I can't be responsible."

"You should have done it in the closet."

"What? And mess it up more than we already did?"

"Just keep moving."

Our progress was slow, though not slow enough to
suit me. Whitney had hardly said a word since the closet
door opened, and I wondered if she was in shock. June,
please come! Please!

Abruptly Barnett stepped around in front of us, gun
levelled. "Okay," he said. "There's your restroom. I'll wait
right here. Now hurry it up."

I looked at the door labelled "Women" and back at
Barnett. "Thank you," I said.

When the door closed softly behind us and I had found
and snapped on the lights, I thought we should try to find
a weapon, a way out, a way to lock the door . . . but we
did have urgent business to attend to first. That taken care
of, things suddenly looked a little brighter. I understood
for the first time the true meaning of the phrase, "to re-
lieve oneself."

"Now," I told Whitney, "let's see what we can do for
you, first."

"God, T.D., I'm so sorry!"

"Me, too, but what we have do now is figure out what
to do. Let's get that ankle tied, up, anyway."

"What with?" she asked reasonably.

I thought, but could come up with no good suggestion, until Whitney answered her own question. "How
about tearing my shirt in strips? That ought to work."

"Wouldn't that leave you topless? He's not going to
like that, conventional as he is."

"Exactly. Look, he's obviously going to take us out
of the building with him, right? So what better way to
discourage that than to have me half-naked? He couldn't
even hope to be inconspicuous!"

This made sense. If we were being held hostage until
Barnett had made some kind of getaway, this would make
him think twice about taking us out in public. He might
abandon us in the building, maybe lock us up again, but
that would be far preferable to most other alternatives that
came to mind. I couldn't really think he planned to kill
us . . . could he?

"Quick, then, before he comes looking for us," I said.
Whitney pulled her shirt off and started ripping it into
strips and handing them to me to tie together.

"We should have brought the scissors," she said. "Then
we could have stabbed the bastard."

"I'm not sure they would have been a match for that
gun, anyway."

"But we could have tried."

I shuddered at the idea of bloodshed. Then it occurred
to me that it was our own blood in danger of being shed.
No. No, that just couldn't happen. Oh, June, please, please
come!

The T-shirt material made a fairly acceptable emergency substitute for an elastic bandage, and I wrapped it
tightly, hoping it would give her at least a modicum of
support to enable her to put some weight on that foot.

"Hurry up in there!" Barnett's voice came to us through
the door, and I called, "Just a minute."

The bandage in place, I helped Whitney hobble to the
door, then, a thought occurring to me, I left her balancing
there and returned to turn on the water in the hand basin
farthest from the door, plugging up the drain as well as I
could with a wad of paper towels. "There," I whispered.
"At least that ought to give somebody the idea that someone was up here today."

I devoutly hoped we would be safely out of our predica-
ment long before anyone discovered the flood, but at this
point I wouldn't have laid any bets.

Barnett's reaction, when Whitney emerged shirtless,
was one of flabbergasted rage. "What the *fuck* do you think
you're doing?" he shouted. Then, lowering his voice, he
went on, berating us for being stupid and indecent and

thinking we were clever, and ended by ordering us back to the office, where he threw the plaid jacket at Whitney and said, "Put that on and march! Out the door. You think you're so smart."

"Ross," I said reasonably, "we had to tie up her ankle so she could walk."

"You had to, yeah. And I guess nobody's going to think a thing about a naked gal on campus on a Sunday night? Give me a break."

"What are you going to do with us?" Whitney said, breaking silence.

"Just keep walking. Down the stairs and turn right."

"I do think," I said, "that you at least owe it to us to tell us what's going on."

"Nothing you need to worry about. Just keep moving and don't make me hurt you, damn it."

Why couldn't this be a building with a library in it, or a lab, like the one at Tech where I used to meet my friend? Then maybe someone, anyone, would be around, would hear us or come around the corner and see us . . . . Our footsteps echoed back from emptiness.

"Ross," I tried again, "you're obviously an intelligent man—"

The blow across my shoulders was staggering. I supposed he had hit me with the gun, but it might have only been his hand. The effect was the same, in any case. After an involuntary cry, I clamped my lips together. Let him cool down a bit, I told myself, fighting panic. I can make him reason with me, but he needs to settle down first. Better just to keep quiet for a little while. We made it to the bottom of the stairs and turned right.

The back door of the building was ahead of us at the end of a dark, narrow hallway. Barnett made us stand back in the shadow against the wall while he unlocked the door, stuck his head out, and looked around quickly. I had the unreal feeling that we were in a T.V. movie. The illusion was spoiled, however, by the smarting of my shoulder where Barnett had hit me just now and the dull ache where his gun barrel had fallen earlier, as I had tried to walk out of the office. Whitney and I caught each other's hands and squeezed hard.

"Outside," Barnett said, turning to us and motioning with his gun. "Walk naturally and don't try anything. At this point I would have to shoot you if you did anything stupid. Get in the car, both of you."

My Mustang waited at the curb where, much earlier, I presumed, the bus bringing June home had stopped. Now no one was anywhere in sight. It must be very late. June, where are you? Oh, June!

"You drive, Dr. Renfro. Whitney, wait while I get in the back. Okay, now — into the passenger seat." I had slid behind the familiar wheel, Barnett had climbed into the back seat, and now it remained for Whitney to get in beside me.

"Come on!" Barnett's voice was a hoarse whisper.

"I'm not getting in that car." Whitney stood beside the door, then took a hobbling step backward.

"Do I have to knock your friend in the head, or what?" Barnett hissed at her. "Now get in, or I'll cold-cock her with this pistol butt, and you, too. I ain't woofin', girl."

Carefully, awkwardly, favoring her ankle, Whitney got in.

"Okay, that's better," said Barnett with relief in his voice. "Doctor, drive straight out to the street there and hang a left. Take it slow and don't attract any attention, because if you do, people are going to get hurt."

I started the car and drove. Why, I wondered, did the car have to cooperate so well? Why couldn't it have failed to start, just this once? The engine purred like a kitten, and I cursed it under my breath.

"What are you muttering about?" Barnett wanted to know.

"The car. I don't like the way it's running."

"It sounds okay to me. I didn't have any trouble with it."

"Well, it doesn't sound right to me. What did you do to it, anyway?" I let annoyance creep into my voice.

"Nothing. Just drove it a little ways and hid it for a while."

"Well, whatever you did, there's something wrong now. Can't you feel that?"

"Feel what? I don't feel anything."

He was getting concerned or exasperated; I was not sure which.

"Well, *I* feel it. Don't you, Whitney? You drove it yesterday; did it run this rough?"

"No. It didn't. It sounds different, too."

"Shut up, both of you!" Barnett was getting fed up. "This little script has gone on long enough. There's nothing the matter with the damn car, and if there is, you can just drive it until it conks out, so shut up."

"I still think we ought to see what's wrong," I said.

"What's wrong is you're talking too damn much!"

"Ross, we're doing what you want us to do. You can't really blame me for worrying about my car, when I don't know what you've done to it or how far you're planning for us to go in the middle of the night without even a service station open, probably—"

"We're going out to the woods and let Whitney tell me again what she thinks she saw, that's all."

"I told you what I saw," Whitney said.

"GOD DAMN IT, SHUT UP!" The gun barrel jabbed the back of my neck and then veered toward Whitney. Without discussing the matter between us, she and I each decided independently that it might be best not to antagonize an armed murderer further at this juncture.

We shut up.

Chapter 22

I followed Barnett's directions, making our way down untraveled side streets, past houses whose lights looked warm and homey, past an occasional pedestrian enjoying the soft evening air, a couple or a solitary person sitting on a front porch here and there, a few cars whose occupants paid us no attention at all. What would you think, I mused, looking at two men conversing in the street beside a parked pickup truck, if you knew a man in my car was holding us at gunpoint?

For that matter, if I turned into one of these driveways, what could Barnett do? I took my foot off the gas when I saw a lighted house ahead, but immediately the hard steel muzzle of the revolver pressed into my neck at the hairline. I drove on. Streets gave way to a country road. Houses thinned; forests rose darkly on either side.

I should have acted before now. I should have rammed a parked car. That's what I should have done. He would have been helpless then; people would have come. We would have been safe. But somehow it doesn't occur to one to wreck one's classic Mustang deliberately, and one doesn't do one's most creative thinking with a gun in one's neck.

The night was dark. If there was a moon, it wasn't shedding any light that I could see. It might be overcast, for all I had noticed. Dark night for dark deeds. I began to recognize a kind of fear I had never felt before, a true, animal fear, the fear of impending death.

Whitney in the passenger seat was staring ahead through the windshield, shoulders drawn in toward her chest, hands in her lap, perfectly still. I took a hand off the wheel with an effort, so tightly did I find my own fingers clenched, and, reaching over, patted her knee. She gripped my hand convulsively.

"Keep your hands on the wheel!" Barnett's voice made me jump.

"This isn't doing you any harm, Ross," I said. I left my hand where it was.

We drove for what seemed like hours. It could only have been a few minutes, really, because when Barnett told me at last to turn, I recognized the road. It was the one which led to the house of Whitney's Uncle Jimmy and Aunt Louise, and just past that to the infamous deer lease.

The scene of the crime, I thought. The scene of one crime. Please, all you Higher Powers that be, please don't let it be the scene of another tonight.

Barnett told me to pull into the driveway there. The gap gate, I thought. He'd have to get out to open it. I could never open it by myself. The three of us would have to separate here, just for a minute, unless he got Whitney out of the car, too. But he'd have to do that to get out of the back seat, himself, unless he slid over and got out my side. I squeezed Whitney's hand, trying to telegraph the message to be ready for action. This might be our last chance.

But the gate was open, its posts and wire pulled aside.

"Keep on," Barnett said. "Just follow this road."

I did as I was told.

What a good girl you are, Daisy. You do as you're told. You should always do as you're told. We're so proud of you when you're good, when you mind your mama, when you do as you're told, as your mama tells you, as your daddy tells you, as your teachers tell you, as the Bible tells you, as your boss tells you, as the government tells you, as the policeman tells you, as the man with the gun tells you, the man with the gun, the man with the gun, the man with the gun. Be a good girl and everybody will love you and you won't get hurt, if you do what he tells you, the man with the gun.

The sandy road twisted and the ruts grabbed at my tires. I slowed, then slowed some more, peering into the darkness at the far reach of the headlights.

It had been a dark night outside on the road; in here, under the pines, it was black as the pit. Individual tree trunks and leafy bushes showed stark in the headlights, then vanished into the darkness behind us as if they had ceased to exist. The road twisted. I wrestled the wheel. It seemed to go on forever. Then Barnett's voice said, "Okay, pull in here," and at the same time I saw the road widen into a flat, clear area with no trees beyond it, only a few upright posts in a short, double row leading into the dark close by. The pier, and the river's edge.

"Let's all get out." His voice was quiet, almost reverent in the pine-scented darkness.

I opened the door, looking at Whitney in the yellow dimness of the interior light, seeing her look at me with mute appeal and manage a thin smile. "Have you ever been in the woods at night, T.D.?" she said in a childlike voice.

"No, I haven't."

She squeezed my hand. "It's nice. Peaceful. It isn't scary."

I returned the pressure of her hand, then turned away and got out, followed by Barnett and his gun. He walked me around to Whitney's side of the car and I helped her out. He pushed the door closed, and the light in the car went out.

The night was full of small sounds, insects, I supposed, and probably frogs, being here by the river as we were. I listened, hoping to hear even the farthest human voice or laughter, but this night in this place belonged to those who lived here, the smaller creatures. Whitney and I were alone, two good girls minding the man with the gun.

"Were you in the Girl Scouts, Whitney?" Barnett asked conversationally.

"Yes."

"Good for you. Here." He handed her something which he must have brought with him from the car. I couldn't see what it was.

"What's this for?" Her voice was high and fearful.

"You'll need to tie up your friend for a few minutes. I can't watch her very well in the dark and I don't trust her not to get in bad trouble."

"Tie her up?"

"Just tie her hands behind her. I'm going to check the knot, so do it good."

"Why do you want her tied up?"

"So she won't try anything that'll make me have to hurt her."

"What could I do?" I asked.

He laughed, almost a bark. "If I tell you, you'll do it!"

"I don't see what threat I could be to you out here. There's no one in miles, and you have the gun. Now, why don't we just sit down, Ross, and talk about this? I know your feelings must be very confusing right now. Sometimes just talking about it helps—"

"No!" He almost shouted it, then dropped his voice and repeated, "No, I don't need my head shrunk, but I do need your mouth shut. Now, shut up, or I'll gag you, too. Whitney, tie her hands like I told you."

So Whitney tied my hands.

"Good and tight, now," Barnett said.

I held my wrists as far apart as I dared while Whitney wrapped the thin rope around them and tied what felt like an elaborate knot. Actually, I had quite a bit of slack, if I could only disguise that fact when Barnett checked the lashings. "Ow!" I cried. "You don't need to do that good a job!"

"Sorry," Whitney said.

Barnett felt the knot with his fingers while I strained to keep the rope tight without letting him feel the space between my wrists. "Okay," he said.

I smiled secretly. I was sure I could get loose fairly easily.

"Now you get down to the dock, both of you," he ordered. "Go on." He jabbed the gun in my ribs, and then Whitney gave a little cry as he apparently did the same to her. With her hobbling and me walking awkwardly with my bound hands behind me, we made our careful way onto the boards of the pier.

The water of the river gave back the faint glow of the overcast sky, looking slightly lighter than the velvet-black land and the trees on the banks. On this background Uncle Jimmy's fishing boat was a dark, sinister shape.

"Into the boat, doctor."

"What? Get in the boat? How can I get in the boat with my hands tied behind my back?" I stalled frantically. I had never been in a boat in my life smaller than the Bolivar ferry, and that holds sixty cars. I could see myself slipping and tumbling into the snake-infested river, and with my hands tied so I couldn't save myself.

"Just do it."

"But how?"

"Damn it, woman, you're more trouble than you're worth! Sit on the edge of the pier, put your feet in the boat, and just slide in."

"I'm afraid it'll tip over!"

Barnett sighed in exasperation. "Whitney, get down there and help her in. You've been in a boat before, haven't you?"

"Yes."

"Well, good! Get down and put her in the bow, and leave the stern seat for me."

Whitney followed orders. I saw the boat bob alarmingly under her weight, but she kept her footing miraculously, even with the hurt ankle, and her steadying hands guided first my feet and then the rest of me to a sitting position ahead of her. The boat rocked again as Barnett joined us, and then he cast off and pushed out into the stream.

"Where are we going?" Fear had driven out all effort at calm in Whitney's voice. "We'll never make it all the way to Louisiana like this!"

"Who said anything about Louisiana?" Barnett rocked the boat again as he did something with the outboard motor, and then it burbled to life, swinging the head of the boat around and moving us off downstream.

"Then where are we going?"

He didn't answer her. The outboard roared louder, drowning out possible conversation, and we plowed on through the night, the river chuckling and hissing under our feet, the breeze of our passage chilling the cold sweat on my brow. I felt Whitney's hand on my back, bracing and steadying me against the bumping of the boat over the water, and then I felt her stealthily untying the knot at my wrists.

"Sit back!" Barnett's voice cut like a whip. Whitney jerked away from me. I froze with my wrists still held by the rope, but testing showed me I could probably wriggle free quickly enough, if I just knew what to do after that.

The ride went on forever. Didn't people fish at night? I had heard they did. Well, where were they now? Maybe it wasn't a good night for fishing. Maybe they were going to fish us out in the morning, me and Whitney, with bullets in us. June!

The river had widened. Ahead I could make out a spreading sheet of flat water whose banks receded on either side. The motor's roar died away to a watery idle and the noise of our movement through the water died with it. We slowed until we were only drifting with the current.

"Okay." Barnett's voice was flat. "This is the end of the line."

"What do you mean?" Whitney and I had both spoken at once.

"You're going to have a boating accident. Whitney's going to fall out, and you, Doctor Renfro, are going to circle back to pick her up."

"I don't understand. What will that accomplish?"

"You'll see. Whitney, stand up and dive over. You do swim, don't you? We'll be right back."

"Wait a minute," I said. "Whitney, wait. Look, you'd better tell us what the purpose of this is, Ross. There are snakes in there—"

"Oh, for God's sake! Shut up, you stupid dyke! Do you really think . . . ? Oh, the hell with it." Abruptly he stood up, rocking the boat wildly, yanked Whitney to her feet, and flung her sideways into the water. Her flailing arms disappeared in the splash, and then I could make out her head coming to the top and hear her gasping and spitting water.

"Ross, have you lost your mind?" I shouted.

For answer he gunned the engine and the boat turned in a wide circle and headed directly for the spot where Whitney was treading water.

"You're going to run over her!" I screamed.

"No, you are!" The motor wound up to a deafening roar, the front of the boat rising as we picked up speed.

"Whitney, look out!" I saw her head disappear, but I couldn't see how she could get out of the way fast enough. Without thinking at all I jerked my wrists loose from the remaining knot, stood up, windmilling my arms for balance, and half-jumped, half-fell onto Barnett. He yelled as he saw me rise and was starting to stand, himself, when I careened into him. I caught him off balance, his yell of outrage turned into a scream, and he flew out of the boat as I knocked the motor's handle to the side and sent us veering away.

I hadn't felt a bump, so I didn't think Whitney had been hit. How did one stop this thing? But it was simple, and I did it, then steered in a circle with the engine idling. I could see two heads in the water, I thought. I steered toward the nearest, and Whitney's voice cried, "T.D.! Over here!" I shoved the handle to the other side just as Barnett's hand grabbed for the side of the boat. Scooting away, I nearly ran Whitney down, but I slowed in time, she caught my hand, and to my amazement I pulled her in, sopping wet, jacket gone, hair plastered to her head and face, and blessedly safe.

A splashing caught my ear as I was embracing my near-drowned friend. Barnett, swimming fast, was coming up behind us.

"Quick! Get us out of here!" Whitney cried. I gunned the engine as if I knew what I was doing, and the boat's front end rose high as we sped away, Barnett's curses receding in the dark.

"We made it! We made it! We made it!" Whitney said, and then, "You'd better slow down a little so we can see where to go."

She was wasting her breath, however, in admonishing me to slow down. Before I could release the throttle, the engine suddenly stuttered, coughed, and died.

"Oh, Christ," I said. The front of the boat settled and we glided to a stop.

"What's wrong with it?"

"How should I know? It just died. How do you start it?"

"I don't know." But she tried to find out, and so did I. We found out how it was supposed to work; that wasn't hard. But the engine refused to start, and that was that.

"What do we do now?" I asked the universe.

"Where's Barnett?" Whitney asked me.

We both looked back the way we'd come, but neither of us could be sure we saw him, though we both thought we did, swimming not toward us, but toward the nearest shore.

"At least he's not after us at the moment," I said. "Are you all right?"

"Yeah." She pushed strands of wet hair away from her eyes. "He was going to run me down."

"Yes, he was."

"And then probably push you out, too."

"Well, he didn't. He hadn't realized I was untied."

"You saved my life, T.D."

"Not yet. We still have to get back to the car. Unless you know of a better way to get out of here."

Whitney didn't. In the bottom of the boat, groping in the dark, we found two paddles. With Whitney in the front—the bow, she informed me—and me in the back—the stern—we set out, shoving at the water with our clumsy blades like a couple of demented Indians in a most ungainly canoe. If Barnett was much of a swimmer, he would reach the shore and set off on foot for my car, I feared. If he was waiting there when we got back, assuming we ever did, which seemed problematic at this rate of progress, we were as good as dead. But the car was not too far from Whitney's aunt and uncle's house. I gave up thinking and applied myself to propelling the world's heaviest boat.

Chapter 23

That the Angelina River where it flows into Sam
Rayburn Reservoir is a lovely stream, I have no doubt.
That its waters form a silken surface over which boats
glide effortlessly is an illusion, a misconception, and a
dastardly lie. I personally pushed tens of tons of that vis-
cous brown fluid behind me that night, and I can attest
to the fact that boating—I've even heard it called "pleasure" boating—is the hardest, sweatiest, most muscle-
splitting, exasperating work known to man.

Whitney said it would be easier if we paddled closer
to the shore. Perhaps it was; I only know that if the task
had been any harder or required one more erg of energy,
Tahoka Daisy Renfro, daughter of the high, dry plains,
would have made her grave in the watery deep.

It did make a difference when we realized we could
tilt the motor up so that we weren't dragging its lower
parts through the water behind us.

Whitney, apparently exhilarated by her brush with
death, soon launched into a chorus of the Song of the Volga
Boatmen: "Ro-ow, men, row! Ro-ow, men, row! 'Gainst
the cur-rent, ro-ow, men, row!"

This soon changed to the ersatz American Indian ditty,
beloved of Girl Scouts who have doubtless never in their
tender lives labored in a boat, that goes, "My paddle's
keen and bright, Flashing with sil-ver!"—a description
which as far as I was able to see bore absolutely no resem-
blance to that of the crude implements we were presently
wielding—and this was followed in its turn by "Dola,

Dola, Dola," which she explained was an Eskimo song about a seal hunt. In this one our bow paddler would periodically cease her labors to shade her eyes with her hand and peer about into the darkness proclaiming, "Hex-a-cola miss-a-waaaa-na!" This was the Eskimo looking for the seal, it seemed. While the Eskimo looked, the exhausted psychotherapist paddled. I was afraid if the boat stopped, we would never get it going again.

A breeze sprang up and pushed us along the way we were going, the first indication to me that nature was not set on torturing us for a slow eternity. I thought briefly of Ross Barnett crashing through the woods like a Sasquatch on his way to my car, either to steal it for his getaway or to lie in wait for our return and finish the job he had started, but mostly I simply paddled mindlessly. Before it was over I had joined in the singing, and Whitney and I arrived off the pier of our embarkation shouting "Hex-a-cola miss-a-waaaa-na!" until the forests rang.

Nothing is simple about boating. We almost never got the contrary craft maneuvered alongside the pier so that I could at last crawl painfully up onto the boards and tie a rope to one of the posts. Somehow, though, we did that, and I helped Whitney up to stand beside me, leaning with arms across each other's shoulders while we caught our breath. We must have looked like Orphans of the Storm standing there, bedraggled, drooping, Whitney bare to the waist and favoring her bandaged ankle, me with my hair disposed about my head in limp and sweaty ringlets. But we were alive and out of the infernal boat, and my Mustang, my beautiful white 1966 Mustang with the maroon convertible top and the matching leather seats, stood waiting in the clearing with no sign of Ross Barnett.

And it wouldn't start.

"Oh, god, T.D., what now?" Whitney moaned.

I raised an admonitory finger and smiled. Compared with what we had already endured, this was a footling obstacle. Getting out, I raised the hood, felt in the dark and found the thing to unscrew, unscrewed, poked, replaced, re-screwed, climbed back in, and started the car without a word.

"Well, I'm impressed." Whitney looked at me admiringly.

"You didn't suspect me of mechanical talents?"

"T.D.," she replied, "by now, nothing you could do would surprise me."

"Let's go home," I said.

The woods and the forest road, so sinister-seeming when we had come in hours ago, now felt familiar and welcoming. " . . . Compared to the river, anyway," I concluded, voicing the thought to Whitney.

We reached the gate, and I drove straight through, leaving it for other, heftier hands to close. I turned onto the road toward town, and a police car passed us from the opposite direction. In the mirror I saw his brake lights flare red; he made a skidding U-turn, and the lights on top of the car came on, along with the siren.

I pulled to the shoulder and stopped as another car flashing a red spotlight veered across the road and halted inches from my front bumper.

"At long last," I said to Whitney, as four uniformed men, two with guns drawn, swarmed out of the cars and surrounded us. Welcome home to the storybook world, where the blue policeman is your friend.

At the Angelina County courthouse in Lufkin we told our story between gulps of coffee and mouthfuls of egg salad sandwich, the first food either of us had had since breakfast about fifty years ago. Whitney was wrapped modestly in a blanket from the jail and I, feeling cold in the air conditioning at my state of physical exhaustion, shivered until a deputy brought me a blanket, too.

The search was on for Barnett, but I gathered that they had the entire Angelina National Forest to deal with, an area with which the fugitive was intimately familiar. I had no desire to stay here until they found him.

That wouldn't be necessary, the sheriff assured me. June had been notified of our whereabouts and was on her way from Nacogdoches—how, I didn't know, since

I had the car—and Whitney's relatives were even now swarming into the courthouse corridors to retrieve their own.

June, from what I could glean in the confusion, had harassed the law enforcement officials of both Angelina and Nacogdoches Counties until they had probably been ready to put her behind bars, herself. She had, as we found out later, enlisted the aid, first, by a long distance call, of Whitney's lover Marilyn, whom it turned out she knew slightly (and ah, the tangled web of lesbian community, complicated in this case by my not talking about my clients with my lover—she had known who Whitney was as soon as I introduced them) and then, through her, of Whitney's local relations, whose word the East Texas law was more ready to heed than that of a stranger from far-off Austin.

Whitney's mother burst into the room and swept her child into her arms. Her cousin Bob, looking haggard, hovered in the background, flashing me a sheepish smile, and other people I didn't know filled the small room we were in to the bursting point over the feeble objections of the sheriff's men.

Then June was there.

We plunged toward each other through the crowd and clung together laughing and crying and talking at the same time, babbling words of endearment and worry and relief.

Knowing when they were licked, the officers of the law suggested that the abductees go home and get some sleep, and after much hugging the happy crowd dispersed, leaving June to drive me back to Nacogdoches and the bed which had played so large a part in my wistful fantasies over the past eighteen hours. The sun was rising over the deep green pines as we walked, both weaving with weariness, to the car.

In the quiet of our room, June undressed me and bathed me and helped me gently to bed between the smooth, cool sheets, and laying her body protectively against my own, she gathered me into her arms. I snuggled my head between her breasts and slept.

Later we had to deal with going back to Lufkin and making a statement. Barnett had been apprehended stealing a car in Broaddus, the one he had stolen earlier in Etoile having run out of gas. He was in jail in the next county, and when I heard the news, the last tension drained away. I muddled through my statement, waited interminably for it to be typed, signed it, and tottered away on June's arm. Wrapped in the jail blanket, which in the confusion I had neglected to return, I slept most of the way back to Austin.

Chapter 24

June, as it turned out, had never had the slightest doubt that foul play had befallen me.

"When you weren't there at the bus and weren't at the motel, I knew damn well something had happened. Getting the cops to listen was something else again."

It had taken her hours to convince the local authorities to look for me and my car, since Whitney's folks were not inclined to worry until she had had ample time to get back to Austin. When they were finally convinced, however, they had dashed into action.

Cousin Bob, wracking his brains for clues, remembered talking to Ross Barnett before church, mentioned the fact to Uncle Jimmy, and found in that reticent gentleman an ardent supporter of the idea that Barnett was not completely to be trusted. The uncle, it seemed, had harbored suspicions about the legendary fire and its origins ever since the embers had ceased to smoulder. He had tried to reach Barnett at home by phone and, failing to make contact, had even driven there to look for him, but without success. Not abandoning the idea that Barnett could be involved in Whitney's disappearance, he had urged the local sheriff to include a description of him in the bulletins.

In the meantime, Whitney's mother, having taken a shine to June, set up headquarters at her house and insisted my lover stay close at hand in case anything developed. June availed herself of the telephone there to call the sheriff's and police departments of all the towns and

counties for miles around to urge them on. If Barnett hadn't
hidden my car somewhere until after dark, probably the
whole thing would have ended sooner and in a less spec-
tacular manner, but he had apparently secreted it well.
Officers had driven through the deer lease looking for us,
but long before we got there. Barnett, some time between
the search by the law and the time he returned with us
as prisoners, had checked out the place using his own car
and thoughtfully left the gate open to facilitate our later
entry.

His plan, as nearly as we were able to piece it out,
had been to stage a boating accident in which it would
appear that Whitney and I had gone on an illicit joy ride
in Uncle Jimmy's boat, she had fallen out, I had run over
her in trying to rescue her, and I had fallen out and
drowned. My car would be found, as would the boat, eventually. Whitney and I were known to have visited the deer
lease the day before, and it seemed probable that Barnett
was counting on the idea that a lesbian intrigue was going
on between us to clinch the thing in the minds of the locals. It might have worked; in fact, it came much too close
for comfort. He would have had to return and clean up
his office at some point, and I wondered how he would
have explained the hole in the closet wall. But he might
not have had to hurry on that score; the storage room obviously wasn't in daily use. I wondered if anybody had
turned off the water in the restroom yet. I hoped I wouldn't
receive a bill for the flood damages.

The only other clue that might tie him to the deed if
we had been found dead was the plaid jacket Whitney
had been wearing when he dumped her out of the boat.
But that was a slim chance. He had thought it out pretty
well, and it was only chance, I reflected, that had caused
his plan to go awry.

"Chance, hell!" June snorted. "From what you say,
you and Whitney were enough to throw a monkey wrench
in anybody's works!"

We were sitting on the back yard deck by the koi pool,
sipping gin-and-tonics. I had taken another day off, and

it was now Tuesday evening. Roya and Caroline had gotten wind of my adventure and, rather than explain it all yet again over the telephone—it seemed I had done that innumerable times already since our return the previous night—we had asked them over for drinks. June and I were getting a head start while we waited for them.

"I was nearly too much of a good girl for my own good," I said. I told her about some of my thoughts about obeying the one with authority.

"But you disobeyed all the way through it."

"Yes. But it went against everything I'd ever been taught. He was so reasonable, June. 'Don't make me hurt you.' "

"But you saw through him, just the same way you've seen through the lies about religion and politics and women loving women. Probably because you'd already learned to question those things."

She was probably right. In any case, Barnett's two dykes hadn't turned out to be the good girls he'd counted on.

"That UFO picture of his still bothers me," June said.

"I have ceased to worry about sinister UFOs."

"But a lot of people saw something. And Barnett took that picture . . . ."

"Which could have been faked, for all we know. He developed it himself, he said."

"So you think the whole thing is a lot of hogwash."

"I didn't say that. In fact, I've come to believe there must be some truth in it. Most of those people seem quite credible. What I am saying is I'm not going to worry about it any more. Whitney apparently was only a murder witness, not a UFO contactee. I'll leave the rest of it to anybody who cares to explore it."

"What do you mean, 'only a murder witness'? Isn't that enough?"

I took a sip of my drink. "I mean, from what I've found out, UFO contact, or whatever it is that's happening to all those people, is at least as dangerous as what happened to us. It's certainly psychologically damaging, and maybe physically, too."

"Not more physically damaging than being run over by a boat, I shouldn't think!"

"You may have something there."

"Well," June conceded, "at least Barnett isn't likely to come back and grab her again, the way UFOs are supposed to do."

"And nobody's going to call her a crackpot and hound her to death, either. I've wondered if it isn't that, as much as anything, that makes some of the contactees' health so bad."

"If that were so, half the dykes and gays would die young."

"Maybe we're tougher."

June looked at me with a sudden tenderness. "You've certainly proved yourself in that department."

I put down my drink and reached for her hand. "The contactees are mostly isolated, as so many of us used to be."

"And a lot of us still are."

"Yes, but not the way we used to be. When I was growing up, I thought I was the only one like me in the world. Now there's even a Gay Students Alliance at Texas Tech. We're finding each other, and it's saving our lives and keeping us whole. I'm not sure I could have come through without Whitney there —or without knowing you were out there somewhere, too." I smiled. "Maybe what makes us tough is love."

"Even if some of us are sometimes tough to love?" she said with a twinkle in her eye.

I drew myself up and fixed her with a reproving gaze. "I hope you are excepting present company from that rather negative assertion," I said.

She laughed and kissed me.

Roya and Caroline made their entrance about then. June got them drinks, we settled around the pool, and I embarked once more on the harrowing tale of the Fearsome Forester and the Dare-devil Dykes. Roya listened with intent interest, silently, but participating with her eyes. Caroline exclaimed and asked questions.

"So when will you have to go back to talk to the grand jury?" she wanted to know.

"I don't know yet. They'll call me."

"And you'll have to testify at the trial?"

"Unless he plea-bargains, they tell me."

"Well, Roya and I feel that you'll need appropriate clothing when you go to testify, so we've brought you a little something." Roya smiled and produced a small package which she had managed to spirit in and hide behind her chair.

"We saw this today and just knew it was you."

I tore off the paper and unfolded a T-shirt. It bore on the front a picture of a racing shell in the water and the legend, "Just Say Row."

☆ ☆ ☆

"I'll miss you when you go." I looked down at June in my arms, tracing with my eyes the lovely, familiar lines of her body. Her eyes looked back at me, serious, unblinking, seeing, it seemed, into my soul.

"I'll miss you, too."

"What will happen to us?"

"I don't know." We were silent. "I know I love you, T.D."

"I know I love you."

"Make love to me again?"

I lowered my face toward hers. Her lips parted; her eyes closed. The future with its danger and its promise swirled far, far away.

Books From Banned Books

The Contactees Die Young,
Antoinette Azolakov $8.95
Skiptrace,
Antoinette Azolakov $8.95
Cass and the Stone Butch,
Antoinette Azolakov $8.95
The Assistance of Vice,
Roslyn Dane $8.95
Lovers,
Tee Corinne $7.95
Dreams of the Woman Who Loved Sex,
Tee Corinne $7.95
Ripening,
Valorio Taylor $8.95
These Lovers Fled Away,
Morgan Graham $8.95
Profiles Encourage (Nonfiction),
Pamela S. Johnson $8.95
Like Coming Home: Coming-Out Letters (Nonfiction),
Edited by Meg Umans $7.95
Death Strip,
Benita Kirkland $8.95
Fairy Tales Mother Never Told You,
Benjamin Eakin $5.95
The Gay of Cooking Cookbook,
The Kitchen Fairy (distributed for Fairy Publications) $10.95

These books are available from your favorite bookstore or by mail from:

Banned Books

Number 231, P.O. Box 33280, Austin, Texas 78764

Add $1.50 postage and handling for one (1) book. For more than one book, add 10% of order total (minimum $1.50, maximum $3.00). Texas residents, please also add 8% sales tax. Send your name and address for our free current catalog and to be added to our confidential mailing list.